SPARK

Also by Mitch Johnson

POP!

SPARK

MITCH JOHNSON

Orion

ORION CHILDREN'S BOOKS

First published in Great Britain in 2022 by Hodder & Stoughton

1 3 5 7 9 10 8 6 4 2

Text copyright © Mitch Johnson, 2022

The moral rights of the author have been asserted.

A CIP catalogue record for this book
is available from the British Library.

Typeset in Berkeley by Avon DataSet Ltd, Alcester, Warwickshire

ISBN 978 1 51010 763 2

Printed and bound in Great Britain by Clays Ltd, Elcograf, S.p.A.

The paper and board used in this book are made
from wood from responsible sources.

MIX
Paper from
responsible sources
FSC® C104740

Orion Children's Books
An imprint of Hachette Children's Group
Part of Hodder & Stoughton Limited
Carmelite House
50 Victoria Embankment
London EC4Y 0DZ

An Hachette UK Company
www.hachette.co.uk

www.hachettechildrens.co.uk

For Evie and Olive

1

The children stood at the water's edge, clutching stones they itched to throw. They watched the boy in the water, squinting against sharp flashes of reflected sunlight, squeezing the sweat from their eyes with slow, stinging blinks. Beads cut tracks across the grubby skin of their faces – faces framed by tangles of shaggy, shoulder-length hair – and dripped on to their shapeless woollen smocks.

The boy in the water waded deeper, sending a ripple across the pool. The children edged backwards as it broke on the stony bank. Their fingers tightened around their rocks.

'You're a 'bomination!' one of them shouted.

'Cursed!'

'A disgrace to the Ancestors!'

The boy dived beneath the surface. The heckling became muffled, distant – echoes from a bad dream on waking – and the fierce heat was soothed by an otherworldly coolness. He opened his eyes but could not see the bottom. It went all the way to the centre of the world, the stories said. It went on for ever.

The boy's lungs soon began to burn. Even here, in the cool gloom of the pool, the sensation was never far away. He reached out for a branch suspended in the water, grabbed it, and kicked for the surface. The heat hit him the moment he broke through; it was like being crushed beneath something vast and immovably heavy. The children's insults filled his ears again, but they dared not throw their stones just yet. Water was holy. They loved the water and they feared it, but above all they knew what happened to those who defiled it: exile.

And exile meant death.

The boy glided to the far bank, and his swimming was like an evil magic to them.

'Witchcraft!'

'Traitor!'

'Four Fathers curse you!'

He climbed out of the far side of the pool and set the branch down on a pile of debris: twigs and wool and strands of sickly yellow grass. He could feel the children watching him – weighing their stones, judging the distance – but knew they would not risk a rock falling short. He was safe, for the time being at least, but the world was full of rocks and children eager to throw them. And there was only one pool.

The children suddenly fell silent. The boy looked up and saw someone walking down from the House on the Hill. She wore a heavy crimson cloak despite the heat, and her long red hair shone like a rare and precious metal. Sheep lumbered out of her way, bleating and huddling together on the sun-baked slope.

The boy quickly scanned the surface of the pool for anything he might have missed before pulling on his rough woollen shirt. His long hair was still damp, but his skin was already dry.

The children dropped their stones at the sight of the approaching figure and retreated, back towards the village. One of them stopped by the stream that fed the pool and stared at the boy with eyes made mean by the sun. The boy recognised him. He was Doran, son of Kelly: the village slaughterman. He was six years old – maybe seven. Without seasons, it was difficult to know for sure.

'One day, Ash,' Doran said, 'you won't have that *witch* to protect you.'

He spat, and the blob of thick phlegm landed dangerously close to the pool. There was no greater insult, in a place where people barely had saliva enough to swallow, than to be spat at. *To cry is a crime, to spit is a sin*, as the old saying went. Doran smiled, then turned to follow the others, towards the grey stone buildings further along the valley floor.

Ash breathed deeply, trying to cool his rage, but the air was thick and hot and full of anger. He wanted to shout – to retaliate – but knew it would only make things worse. Years of being the most hated person in Last Village had taught him that. He'd learned long ago that you ran when you could and fought when you couldn't. The rest of the time you kept your head down and your mouth shut and hoped to go unnoticed.

A mosquito whined around his head. It made him think of his mother, dead to the blood sickness, and he couldn't think of his mother without thinking of his father, dead to the village. Dead to everyone except Ash. Every night he prayed to each of the Four Fathers for an answer, for some kind of sign that proved the villagers were wrong. But the Ancestors were cruel. They gave him nothing, and it was hard not to interpret *that* as a sign; perhaps they gave him nothing because he deserved nothing. Perhaps he was the son of a deserter after all.

'You are thinking of him, aren't you?'

Ash flinched and turned to find the woman in the crimson cloak directly behind him. He dipped his head and clasped his hands. 'Who, Priestess?'

'Your father.'

Ash looked up – failed to stop himself – and saw the thin smile on her lips.

'Don't look so surprised. I can always tell when you're thinking of him.'

'How?'

'You think of little else.' The Priestess lifted her eyes to watch the retreating children. 'You are permitted to think of little else.'

Ash felt the shame of his father's legacy, the shame of being who he was, and returned his gaze to the ground.

'You are not your father, no matter how much you might resemble him.' The Priestess removed her cloak. Ash held out his arms and felt the scratchy weight of it against his skin. 'And even if you were, there are far worse people to be.'

Ash looked up but the Priestess had already stepped past him, towards the pool. She wore a long pale gown, and it darkened as she entered the water. She caressed the surface with her fingertips. When she reached the point where the slope fell steeply away, she swam towards the head of the pool, where the stream poured in with such a delicious, delicate sound.

The Priestess turned on to her back, closed her eyes, and began to stream-dream.

Until recently, this ritual had taken place every seventh day. But for the past few weeks, the Priestess had taken to communing with the Ancestors almost daily. Ash did not mind – clearing the pool provided a break from the heat, as well as protection from the others – but he knew enough about the Ancestors to know it was not a good omen.

He watched the Priestess float on the surface of the pool, her red hair fanned around her head in a wide circle, wondering what visions and whispers she received from the deep. She looked like something fantastical, like one of the sea creatures in her books from the Olden Days. Ash looked south, over a rocky wasteland that led, supposedly, to the ocean. He had never seen it himself: it was a five-day trek, and nobody trekked for five days and returned to tell tales about it.

That was what his father had done, some people said. Others said he'd gone north, to the Kingdom. That was a kind way of saying he was dead. The Kingdom was real in the same way that the Ancestors were real: there but not there. Nobody knew if it was the kind of place you could find with a heart still beating in your chest. It didn't really matter. His father had committed the worst crime imaginable: he had left his post and abandoned the village. The shame for Ash was twofold: not only had his father deserted his people, he'd been left behind by the very person supposed to protect him.

Ash felt sharp little claws of heat scurry across his scalp. He did not believe the stories people told about his father, and he did not think that the Priestess believed them either. Why else had she defended Ash at his trial? Why else had she offered to take him in as her servant? Why else did she tell him that he resembled his father, and not mean it as an insult?

Ash looked north, at the little stone houses nestled in the valley, and thought of the people who lived there – people who despised him. People who had called for him to be sent into the wilderness after his father. *The branch doesn't fall far from the tree*, they had said. He knew it would not be long until the men began to throw punches at him as well as insults. He was almost of age, after all.

A gasp and a splash drew his attention back to the pool. The Priestess looked around, as though she had emerged from an underwater labyrinth into a strange and frightening place. She swam quickly to the shallows and walked out, water dripping from her hair and gown. The droplets hit the dry, dusty stones with little hisses. Something about the way her gown clung to her lithe body, or the lankness of her hair, or the troubled expression on her face, suddenly made the Priestess seem frail. Ash realised, for the first time, how old she must be. Forty, at least. Maybe even as old as forty-five. And how many people made it to fifty? Not many.

He held up the heavy cloak, and the Priestess slipped it on. She trudged up the hill, and it seemed much more of a struggle than it ever had before. Ash watched her climb, and as he did so he remembered Doran's threat.

One day, you won't have that witch to protect you.

The Priestess was the only person who stood between him and exile, but some day she would be gone.

And how long will I last then? he thought, setting off after her. *How long will I last then?*

2

Ash brought a fresh pot of ink into the back room, his fingers black and reeking of charcoal. As he set it down on the corner of the table he caught a glimpse of the almanac open before the Priestess. The pages were crinkled with damp and yellow with age, but the markings she made were bold and precise. A series of circles arced across the right-hand page, each one surrounded by cryptic symbols and annotations. As he lingered, the Priestess dipped the nib of her pen into the ink and added another stroke to the intricate diagram.

'Thank you, Ash.'

Ash bowed his head and stepped silently across the stone floor. He stopped at the door, uncertain, and the Priestess sensed his hesitation.

'You wish to say something?'

Ash swallowed. It was not his place to ask questions – not his place to do anything other than serve – and yet he found himself asking all the same. 'What did they say while you were in the pool? The Ancestors? Are they going to lift the curse?'

The Priestess set her pen down beside the book and stared at the sickly candle on her desk. 'We are at a point of great change,' she said. 'Whether that change is for the better or for the worse remains to be seen. It may be many generations before the Four Fathers are satisfied that we have suffered enough.'

Ash remained by the door. He could smell the queasy stench of mutton fat from the pot of stew beginning to boil in the next room. He knew he should tend to it, but he did not like cooking. Cooking made a hot house hotter. 'How will we know when we have suffered enough?' he asked.

The Priestess half turned in her chair. Her hair caught the candlelight and shone like fire. 'When the Ancestors give us a sign.'

'What kind of sign?'

The Priestess had never been unkind to Ash, but he was fearful of her response all the same.

'Come here,' she said, simply.

Ash obeyed. He stood beside the table once more, looking down at the beautiful sketches in the almanac.

The Priestess picked up her pen, dipped it in the pot, and began to fill a circle at the edge of the page with ink.

'For many years, since long before you were born, I have been watching the sky. In particular, I have been watching the sun and the moon.' She inked her nib and continued to fill the circle. 'There is a pattern to the sky, if you watch it closely enough, and for long enough.'

The circle was now black, and the Priestess took a moment to admire it. 'In three days' time, I predict that the sun will disappear.'

Ash swallowed. He looked at the black spot on the crinkled page. He wiped a hand across his forehead, leaving a dark smudge on his skin.

'If it comes to pass, that will be the sign,' the Priestess said.

'And things will get better after that?'

'The sun is the cause of our misery. If it disappears – as my studies and the Ancestors have led me to believe it will – then we will enter a new age. The seasons will return, and with them will come the animals, and the plants, and the rest of life.'

'What if it doesn't come back? The sun, I mean?'

The Priestess smiled. 'It will come back. The Ancestors will extinguish its light for only a few moments.'

'But if it doesn't?'

Ash realised that he was close to blasphemy. The Priestess spoke for the Ancestors here on Earth. If she said it was so, it was so. But still. The sun had been such a fierce presence in Ash's life, glaring down at everything he did, that it was impossible to imagine even a moment without it – this miniature night-in-day she spoke of.

'It will come back,' the Priestess said, with another smile.

Ash bowed his head. 'Yes, Priestess. Four Fathers be praised.'

'And may they always guide you.'

Ash dipped his head again and turned to leave. He had barely taken a step when a fist hammered against the door of the house. He looked to his mistress. Visitors after dark were rare – night storms swept in too fast to make it safe, and to disturb the Priestess was to disturb the Ancestors. But the Priestess was not fazed. She simply closed the ledger and laid her pen upon it. It seemed to Ash that she had known the interruption would come.

'You should see to the stew,' she said, rising to her feet. 'Our guests will be hungry.'

'Yes, Priestess.'

Ash followed her into the next room: low and wide and sparsely furnished. A wooden table sat across from the roaring fireplace, where a black cauldron bubbled and dripped and fizzed. The flames brushed the flagstone floor with golden light, but the corners remained deep and dark.

The knocking came again, loud and impatient.

Ash stirred the stew, watching as the Priestess glided towards the stout wooden door. She placed her fingers on the iron ring, paused, and then pulled it open.

'Dain,' she said, her voice calm and dreamy. 'Come in. I have been expecting you.'

A stocky man with a black beard lumbered into the room. His dark woollen tunic was fastened across his chest with knucklebone buttons, and his sheepskin boots were encrusted with dirt. He gazed about the room and when his eyes fell on Ash, his scowl deepened.

But Ash was not looking at the man. He was looking at the girl he pushed into the room ahead of him. She was small and slight and wary. She stole a glance at the fireplace – at the pot bubbling there – and quickly looked at her grubby boots. The shadow cast by her straggly hair made it hard to tell, but it looked as though her face was bruised.

That wasn't the most striking thing about her, though. What made Ash stare was the fact she did not belong to Last Village. She had come from somewhere else.

'Caught her sneaking in,' Dain said. 'I was on watch at the Northern Post when she come creeping along the stream, under cover of darkness. Would have made it, too, had I not collared her.'

The Priestess did not look at Dain, to his obvious displeasure. She looked at the girl. 'We should send for Tristan,' she said. 'This is a matter for the Council.'

'Already done. I sent a boy to rouse him on my way over.' Dain smirked. He seemed pleased to know something the Priestess did not.

'Good. Sit down at the table. Ash will bring you something.'

The Priestess gently closed the door while Dain shoved the girl further into the room. He dropped into one of the three chairs on the far side of the table and stretched his legs out. Ash ladled a portion of stew into a bowl, dipped a cup into the water tub, and took them to Dain, stepping cautiously around the girl. Dain did not wait to be brought a spoon; he cupped the bowl between his hands and slurped it down. Then he took a noisy gulp of water, wiped his mouth with the back of his hand, and belched. He kept his eyes on the girl the whole time.

A few moments later, there was a timid knock at the door. The Priestess opened it to admit Tristan, a rangy man with olive skin and hair the colour of dead grass. His beard was long and unkempt, and he brought the sharp smell of sheep dung into the house with him.

'Priestess,' he mumbled, shuffling further into the room. He nodded at Dain before letting his attention fall on the girl. His eyes narrowed to a squint, creasing the skin around them. 'Who is she?'

'That is what we intend to find out,' the Priestess said. She led Tristan to the table and took her seat in the middle, between the two men.

'Turn to face us then, girl!' said Dain.

The girl flinched and shuffled in a quarter circle. Ash brought water and stew to the table, refilled Dain's bowl, then shrank back into a shadowy corner. He remembered his own trial, the morning after his father failed to return from the night watch at the Northern Post, and his stomach filled with the same twisting unease.

The girl swayed on the spot.

'Stand straight,' Dain said.

Ash saw the girl try, but a moment later she rocked

unsteadily from her heels to her toes.

'Ash,' the Priestess said. 'Please bring a chair for this girl.'

Dain shot the Priestess a contemptuous look. 'She should stand before the Council and the Ancestors,' he said. 'There's nowt wrong with her. She's playing us.'

'She looks to have been beaten,' the Priestess said, her voice dangerously deliberate. 'And quite recently.'

Dain folded his arms on the table top. 'Aye. It's a rough world beyond the boundary, make no mistake.'

Ash returned with a chair and set it down behind the girl. She looked to the Priestess – who nodded once – before lowering herself into it.

'I think a bowl of stew wouldn't go amiss, either.'

Ash dutifully filled another bowl while Dain muttered his disapproval. The stew was no sooner in the girl's hands than at her lips. It dribbled over her chin and ran between her fingers.

'*Savage*,' Dain muttered. 'Are we going to find out who she is now?'

'We are,' the Priestess said. 'But it's equally important to demonstrate who *we* are as well.'

The girl lowered the bowl and held it in her lap.

'What is your name, child?'

The girl swallowed. 'Bronwyn.'

'Strange name,' Dain said. 'Foreign name.'

The Priestess ignored him. 'Where have you come from?'

'North.'

'Well, there's nowt to the south, is there?' Dain said. 'Everybody knows that.'

'Let the child speak.'

The girl glanced nervously at the men bathed in light, then at the woman shrouded in the darkness of her shadow.

'I come from a village called Deddon.'

'Do you worship the Ancestors in Deddon?' Dain asked. 'The Four Fathers?'

The girl looked into her half-empty bowl. 'In our own way, yes.'

'*In your own way.* What's that supposed to mean?'

'We know that our forefathers created this world. That we suffer because of them.'

'That's right. So what are you doing here? Did the chiefs of Deddon send you to spy on us?'

'No. I came here because there was nowhere else to go.' The girl took a quick sip from her bowl, as if she feared it might be taken away from her before she could finish it.

'So you were exiled from your village and you came here expecting us to take you in?' Dain raised a cruel, mocking eyebrow. 'Is that it?'

'I wasn't exiled.'

The Priestess lifted her left hand, silencing Dain before he could reply.

'Why did you leave Deddon, Bronwyn?'

The girl glanced at the door, then seemed to sense Ash in his corner and peered briefly over her shoulder. She looked as he must have done all those years ago: unhappy, alone, scared. Then she turned back to the Priestess. 'I left because Deddon is empty. There's no one there. I came back from a foraging trip and everyone was just . . . gone.'

Dain drew a hissing breath between missing teeth. 'Sounds like you fell foul of the Ancestors. A curse, Priestess? Or a plague, perhaps? What if she's brought it with her?'

The Priestess shook her head. 'That is not the Ancestors' way.' She looked at Bronwyn with an expression of concern. 'Why didn't you go north?'

'I did go north. The next village was abandoned, too. I came south because I knew there was a village here.'

She lowered her head – in shame, in despair. 'I half expected to find it empty – to be the last one left.'

For a long moment, the only sound was the crackling of the fire.

'This isn't right,' Dain said. 'It smells wrong – rotten. We must turn her out.'

'Be quiet,' the Priestess said sharply. 'We are at a crucial point – we are on the cusp of forgiveness. Things will happen in the coming days that may not happen again for a hundred years – longer.'

'What things?' Tristan asked.

'Darkness will fall in the middle of the day – a sign from the Ancestors that our suffering is at an end.'

Neither of the men spoke. They only looked at the Priestess with hopeful, mistrusting eyes.

'What we do to this girl will be counted for us or against us. You say she is a curse, and I say she is a gift. If we turn our backs on her, we turn our backs on salvation. She has been sent to test our worth. We must not fail.'

'You mean to let her stay?' Tristan asked.

'I do.'

'But where will she stay?' Dain asked. 'And what will she eat? We barely have enough food for our own.'

'She will stay here with me, and she will eat at my table.'

Dain made a noise of disgust. Had he been anywhere else, Ash was certain he would have spat. The Priestess turned on him with a look that Ash had only ever seen once before, when Dain had argued for *his* exile. It was a look that made the sun seem weak and kind.

'If you have something to say, Dain, you had better say it.'

Dain ran a stubby finger around the rim of his bowl. 'I just think you ought to be careful, Priestess. You're building quite the little nest here, what with the *boy* you insisted on keeping.'

Dain's eyes slid to Ash, who felt his cheeks grow hot.

The Priestess spoke softly, but her words were laden with threat. 'Ash is destined for greater things than dying of thirst on a lonely hilltop.'

Ash had never heard the Priestess mention his destiny before. The thought that he had a future – a purpose – beyond being the butt of jokes and the target for thrown stones gave him courage.

Dain held up his hands. 'I don't doubt your wisdom, Priestess. I only wish to speak honestly as an Elder of Last Village.'

'And you have spoken.' The Priestess turned to her right. 'Tristan. What is your opinion?'

Tristan looked very intently at the table top. He seemed determined to avoid Dain's stern gaze. 'I think . . . if the Four Fathers have sent us this girl as a test then we must protect her. Is it really true that the sun will disappear?'

The Priestess nodded.

Tristan ran a hand over his matted hair. 'Very well. I vote against her banishment. But I want her gone if there's any sign that she's cursed.'

'Then the matter is settled,' the Priestess said.

Dain stood up, thrusting his chair back so forcefully that it toppled to the floor. He strode to the door and yanked it open. He glared at the Priestess, and she held his gaze with cool contempt.

'You're making a mistake, Priestess. That girl' – he jabbed a finger in her direction – 'will be the death of us all.'

He left, slamming the door behind him. Tristan flinched as though he'd been struck, but the Priestess didn't so much as blink.

'You should be proud, Tristan,' she said. 'You did a good thing tonight.'

He nodded reluctantly, staring at Bronwyn. 'Then why do I feel like I just doomed the entire village?'

The Priestess led him to the door and smiled reassuringly. 'Because sometimes things have to get worse before they can get better.'

'Four Fathers be praised,' he mumbled.

'And may they always guide you.'

Tristan stepped into the darkness and the Priestess shut the door behind him. Ash saw her shoulders drop, and she rested her hand on the rough wood as though for support.

'I think I will retire,' she said, making her way to the narrow wooden staircase. 'Tomorrow is going to be a difficult day.'

Ash was sent to fetch a blanket for Bronwyn and told to give her as much stew as she could eat. This turned out to be three bowls. She did not speak. She did not look up. She only sipped and chewed.

Ash was glad of her silence. He had no idea what to say to someone from another village; he had never met anyone from beyond the boundary before. To his knowledge, no one had. He knew the watchers sometimes saw people from their vantage point at the Northern Post, but only at a distance. The rumours of marauding

Items that you have returned

Title: The bear who did
ID: C334451346

Title: The princess who flew with dragons
ID: C334391671

Total items: 2
04/08/2022 12:52

Thank you for using self service

Tel 03000 41 31 31

Items that you have returned

gangs were just that: rumours. The Priestess had been beyond the village boundary many times in her youth, but she only spoke of places: forests and lakes and hills. Never people. The only thing that Ash knew for sure was that outsiders were not to be trusted.

And Ash did not trust Bronwyn.

The fire was dying in the hearth, and the girl was becoming less distinct. For the first time, Ash worried about the coming darkness.

What if she's got a knife beneath that shirt? What if she's waiting for the Priestess to fall asleep before slitting her throat?

He raised a hand to his own neck and felt the smooth skin there. His beard had not come yet, and he would not look like the men of Last Village until it did. He swallowed, and no Adam's apple bobbed.

Whoever Adam was. Whatever an apple might be.

'You can sleep over there,' he said, nodding towards the door, far from the comfort of the fire. 'I've put a blanket down.'

Bronwyn looked over her shoulder, turned back. 'Thank you.'

'If you need to go, do it outside – there's a hole around the back.'

Bronwyn nodded.

'And don't go in any other rooms. You are in the house of the Priestess. Do you know what that means?'

Bronwyn gazed at him. In the low light, it looked like a glare. She did not answer.

'It means this place is holy. The Ancestors dwell here. They speak through the Priestess.'

It looked like the girl was grinning, but then a log crumbled in the grate and the smile was gone.

'I am very tired,' the girl said, in a small voice. 'Can I sleep now?'

Ash bit his lip and narrowed his eyes. Then he nodded. The girl got up from the table.

'I'll be watching you,' Ash said.

The girl rested the fingertips of one hand on the table as if to steady herself, then turned away. She crossed the room very slowly. When she lowered herself to the floor, Ash was certain that her legs would buckle before she reached the blanket. But her strength held out. She lay down on her side, her back to the room, and curled into a ball.

Ash went over to his own blanket beside the dying fire. He intended to stay awake all night, watching the strange girl by the door. But as the fire dimmed and darkness fell, he felt himself drifting off. She was just a shape now, a shadow, and shadows were harmless.

And, like a shadow, he suspected she would be gone when the sun rose.

3

Ash realised too late that he was being murdered. He felt her hands on his shirt, his throat, his face. Felt her hot breath on his cheek as he fought to surface from sleep. He became aware of a thudding sound. She hadn't brought a knife – he knew that now with sickening certainty. She had come unarmed, planning to use something from inside the house. Something heavy and blunt and crushing. She shouted, and her voice cut through the murk, loud and breathless and . . .

Panicky?

Ash's eyelids flew open. An eye, bloodshot and swollen and glossy purple, looked down from above. Ash sat up, throwing Bronwyn's hands from his shirt. He looked around.

Brilliant sunlight poured in through the deep, unglazed windows on either side of the door, and an energised hum drifted through on the hot breeze.

'What is it?' he asked.

'They're here,' she said, flinching as a hand hammered on the door.

'Who?'

'All of them.'

Ash scrambled to his feet just as the Priestess swept into the room.

'Go into the back room and close the door,' she said. 'Get Bronwyn to the church. Do not let anyone see you.'

Ash opened his mouth but nothing came out. It was like waking into a nightmare.

'*Now*,' the Priestess said.

It was Bronwyn who pulled Ash into the back room and shut the door.

'Why are they here?' he asked. He suddenly became aware of Bronwyn's hand around his wrist and snatched it away. 'What did you do?'

'Nothing.'

The raised voices outside fell silent as soon as the Priestess spoke. 'People of Last Village, welcome. I know why you have gathered here, and I understand—'

'Come on,' Ash said. He crossed the room and went through the back door. Before him, the ground dipped down to the pool at the end of the village, and a derelict church stood on the hilltop opposite. The sun, still low in the sky, was already hot enough to burn and bright enough to blind. Ash covered his eyes and peered into the empty valley. 'This way,' he said.

They hurried down the steep slope, their feet trampling clumps of brittle grass. A loud voice shouted somewhere above them, and a cheer went up, but they kept moving. Ash knew the Ancestors would not allow the Priestess to come to any harm, but he still feared for her safety, and dreaded to think what the villagers might do when they realised the girl was gone – and that he had helped her to escape.

Sweat trickled across his scalp as the hill began to level off. His breath came in short, painful bursts, but he knew they couldn't stop running until they had reached the safety of the church.

And then he saw something that made him stop dead. And he knew, in an instant, why the villagers had congregated at the House on the Hill.

He saw what Bronwyn had done.

The stream that ran through the village and fed the pool was dry. Dark pebbles that had only ever known the cool kiss of water were pale and dusty. The pool was already being lost to the air, stolen by the sun.

Ash turned to Bronwyn, ready to drag her back to the house and deliver her to the mob, but hesitated. She was staring at the dry streambed in horror, a hand over her mouth.

'The stream,' she whispered.

'Put it back,' Ash said, wiping the sweat from his forehead. 'Make it right again. Go on!'

'What?' Bronwyn stared at him in shock. 'You think I did this? You think I stopped all that water from flowing?'

Ash stared at her, trying to find some telltale sign of her power, but all he could focus on was the bruising around her eye, the fresh cut in her top lip. She was small and wounded and – seemingly – far from the sorceress she would have to be to cause a drought. This was high magic – the stuff of the Four Fathers.

Another ugly, hungry cheer went up above them.

'We have to go,' Bronwyn said. 'If they think I did this . . .'

Ash looked up at the House on the Hill and said a silent prayer to the Ancestors. Then he began the gruelling climb to the church. The heat seemed to intensify the higher they got, and the air felt thick enough to chew. Every step was harder than the last. Their hearts pounded, their lungs burned, and their mouths filled with the taste of blood.

Finally, they reached the summit, and Ash staggered over a tumbledown wall that circled the graveyard. Most of the tombstones had been toppled by storms, but a couple of smooth slabs still stood at jaunty angles. There was a statue, too, although its wings and arms had long since turned to rubble at its feet.

Ash led Bronwyn through a doorless archway and slumped against a wall. The sun had not yet risen high enough to pour in through the broken roof; the stones against which they rested were shady and cool. The floor was dotted with thousands of dark droppings, and yellow tufts of wool clung to broken pieces of masonry. The pews had been broken up and burned in the village long ago – the books too – but there were still shards of wood and scraps of paper amongst the dust and dung.

'Are we safe here?' Bronwyn asked, as soon as she had enough breath to speak.

'For now,' Ash said. 'But if they find out we're not at the house, there are only so many places to hide in the village. And with everyone searching . . .'

Bronwyn swallowed, but her throat was scratchy and dry. The effort made her cough. 'Will that woman – the priestess – tell them where we went?'

'No. She will tell them to go home and pray.'

'And will they listen to her?'

'Of course. She speaks for the Ancestors.' A bead of sweat rolled into Ash's left eye, and he blinked hard to clear his vision. 'If they do come here, I can't protect you. Do you understand that? It will be the will of the Ancestors, and I won't – can't – stand in their way.'

Bronwyn looked at Ash as though he had become one of the statues that lined the walls: a particularly shoddy and weatherworn statue. She looked away. 'I don't expect you to protect me.'

'Good,' Ash said, although he felt far from it.

Bronwyn sat down with her back to the wall. She drew her knees up to her chest and hugged them. 'You can go now. I don't like the thought of your priestess facing that mob alone.'

Ash wanted to leave but couldn't. He felt guilty, conflicted. A small voice in his head told him that he was just like his father, abandoning the person who needed him most. But this was different. This girl was not from here. She had been caught sneaking in and had brought nothing but ill-luck and another mouth to feed. If protecting Last Village was everything, then surely protecting an outsider was the treacherous thing to do?

He did not know what to do for the best, but he knew that the Priestess might need him, and leaving for that reason made him feel slightly less wretched. 'Tristan keeps the sheep in here overnight,' he said. 'You'd be best to hide when he brings them up. There's a small room at the end there, where the holy men used to live.'

Bronwyn nodded, although she didn't move her gaze from the opposite wall.

'I'll bring over something to eat and drink when I can.' The words were out before Ash could stop them, and he felt a sudden, ugly need to ruin them. 'It might not be till tonight.'

Bronwyn nodded. 'Thank you.'

Ash stood in the doorway, knowing that there was something he should be doing or saying to make the situation less unbearable, but completely at a loss as to what that might be. 'Well, goodbye.' He stepped through the archway before he had a chance to witness the effect of his words.

The heat hit him like a punch, and it was a blow he felt he deserved.

He hurried away from the church without a backward glance. The pool seemed even lower now, and he could see from his vantage point that the village was deserted.

As he ascended the slope to the House on the Hill, sweat dripping from his nose and chin, he heard the murmuring crowd, and the Priestess's voice carrying over the hubbub.

'Do not squander our suffering!' she called, just as Ash made his way around the side of the house. Everyone was too enrapt to notice him. 'The girl, the drought, and the coming darkness are the final tests, but we must expect another. Each of the Four Fathers will set a trial.'

'What will it be, Priestess?' Mildred, the slaughterman's wife, called. Her smock was brown and stiff with blood.

'That is not for us to know. Perhaps the final test is uncertainty itself. Whatever it is, do not despair. We cannot afford to fail.'

'What if we moved the girl beyond the boundary?' Quinn, the watcher, asked. He was lean and spoke with a deep voice. 'The stream only ran dry after she turned up.'

Dain had taken up a position near the house, apart from the crowd. He shook his head vigorously. 'That wouldn't be enough. That girl was sent as a test, make no mistake, but the test is whether we will sacrifice her in the Ancestors' honour. If her blood has not been spilled by the time the sun disappears, *our* lives will be forfeit.'

'Hold your tongue, Dain!' the Priestess said.

'I will not.' Dain crossed his arms over his powerful chest. 'I am an Elder of Last Village, and I will not stand by while you let my people perish!'

The Priestess arched an eyebrow. 'You would defy the Ancestors?'

Dain drew in a deep breath through his nostrils. 'No,' he said, after a long pause. 'But I would defy *you*.'

There was a collective gasp from the crowd, and muttering, and it only stopped when Dain made a guttural noise in his throat, leaned forward, and spat on the step below the Priestess. A deathly silence fell.

Dain turned to the villagers. He had their undivided attention. 'For many years, this woman has served as our priestess – communing with the Four Fathers, imparting her wisdom, prophesying. She is a noble lady, and I do not say that she is without power.' He looked at her from the corners of his eyes, like some sly creature that has administered a slow poison. 'She has plenty of that, I'd say. A great deal. And power has an ugly knack of changing people.'

Speak for yourself, Ash thought. His eyes flitted to his mistress, who stood very still, looking down at Dain without blinking. *Why doesn't she stop him?*

Why don't the Four Fathers strike him down?

'So I ask you now,' Dain said, turning back to the villagers, 'are you happy with her governance? She pleads with the Four Fathers every day for an end to your suffering – has done for years, decades. And is your suffering ended? Or has it, over time, grown worse? Is the sun not hotter than in the time of your childhood? Is the land not more sickly? And your bodies – are they not skinnier than they have ever been?' Dain stared hard at the people, and the people stared hard at themselves. 'You are like a walking boneyard, and that is how your priestess likes it. The thinner and weaker you are, the less strength you have to wield against her. The worse your situation, the better hers becomes. She claims to want to end your misery. Well. There are two ways to end someone's suffering.'

He turned to address the Priestess directly. 'But you eat well enough, I dare say. Why, last night I turned up unannounced – having just caught the outsider – and there was a full cauldron of mutton stew just coming to the boil. I doubt any of you have ever seen such a feast – and all for her and the traitor's son, that *boy* she keeps as her pet.'

The crowd tittered and exchanged glances. Someone

near the back spat on the ground.

Ash's fingers curled into fists. The clenched muscles of his jaw began to ache. *Why doesn't she say she knew he was coming? Why doesn't she tell them the stew would have fed us for days?*

But the Priestess held her tongue.

'And that is not the worst of it,' Dain said, wagging a stubby finger. 'She gave the girl a bowl too!' The tittering turned to uproar, and Dain watched with smiling eyes. 'I see you're all beginning to see things the way I see them – as they really are. Surely you've noticed your priestess bathing in the pool every day, while the rest of us must stay away, sweating and toiling and grovelling for every sip of water?'

Stream-dreaming, Ash thought. *Everyone knows she's stream-dreaming*. And yet he saw several people nodding their agreement. Loxley, the weaver, whispered in Kelly's ear. The slaughterman shook his head and fiddled with the cruel club hanging from his waist.

'I am sorry to be the one to lift the wool,' Dain said. 'Truly I am. But the so-called "Priestess" is leading us to our doom. She is harbouring an outsider – a *cursed* outsider – in this very house. Protecting the girl over all of you! Over all of us!'

No, Ash thought. He wanted to shout it, to scream it. But he knew his words were worthless. If he spoke up for the Priestess, he would only condemn her further. All he could do was stand and seethe and feel his hatred for Bronwyn burrow deeper.

If I give her up, I could become a hero.

But no sooner had the thought crossed his mind than he saw the Priestess looking directly at him, and he knew the thought would go unspoken. To betray Bronwyn would be to betray the Priestess.

Dain raised his hand, and the crowd fell silent in a way it had only ever done for the holy woman. 'Last night, I argued for the girl to be cast out. I warned that she would bring nothing but misfortune.' He shook his head. 'But I was voted down. The Priestess and Tristan united against me. I respect our customs, and so I had no choice but to accept the Council's verdict. But the decision weighed heavily on my conscience. I barely slept last night, and today I woke to this.'

He held his arms out, as though the whole world was changed.

The crowd turned their scowling faces towards Tristan, who lowered his wiry yellow head.

'But Elder Tristan voted under a particular condition,'

Dain continued. 'He said that he would change his mind should there be any sign that the girl was cursed. Isn't that so, Tristan?'

Tristan glanced at Dain, cringing against the clot of hate at his back. 'Aye. That's so.'

'And I think it would be fair to say there was a certain amount of coercion in the way you voted. Letting the girl stay didn't seem to sit well with you.'

Tristan looked at Dain more steadily. He glanced around and began to nod, slowly at first but then with more assurance. He understood that he was being offered a path to safety – and he lunged for it.

'The Priestess is a very persuasive woman,' he said, raising his head and setting his shoulders. 'I didn't feel like myself last night.' He glanced at Dain, who nodded encouragingly. 'In fact, I wondered afterwards whether I hadn't been preyed upon by some sort of witchcraft.'

The crowd took a panicky step backwards. Those at the front tried to ease behind their neighbours. Ash saw a child being snatched into the folds of its mother's skirt.

'Do you wish to change your mind?' Dain asked. 'Any vote may be recast if it's the Elder's will – especially if they've since broken free from some kind of hex.'

'I do,' Tristan said, his voice loud and firm.

'You wish for the girl to be banished?'

'Aye.'

Ash closed his eyes and shook his head, trying hard to ignore the flood of relief he felt.

'Very well,' Dain said. He turned to the Priestess. 'Will you go inside and fetch the girl?'

The Priestess raised her chin. 'I will not.'

A hiss of disapproval rippled through the crowd.

'In which case I shall have to come in and take her.'

Dain stepped towards the door, but the Priestess refused to move.

'This is a holy house. The Four Fathers dwell here. I will not permit force to be used within its walls.'

Dain hesitated. The mention of the Four Fathers had momentarily unnerved him. He looked up at the small, deep windows, dark even in the fierce morning light. They were like empty eye sockets, and yet they seemed to see all.

'You intend to disobey the will of the village?' he said.

'No. I do not. The will of the village is to survive – more than survive: to live. If you take this girl now, the Ancestors will see that we are duly punished. Our suffering will not end. It will worsen.' She took a deep breath and looked out over the villagers. 'In three days' time, the sun will disappear and our suffering will be over. If that does not come to pass, you may banish me in the girl's place.'

'No!' Ash shouted, but his voice was lost amongst the noise of the crowd.

Dain's eyes lit up with a cruel hunger, but he waited for the hubbub to subside before speaking. 'Banishment won't be enough to appease them, Priestess. What the Ancestors demand is a sacrifice. Blood. Will you take the girl's place then?'

The Priestess looked down at her clasped hands. 'I will.'

There was no response from the villagers. No whispers, no shouts. They stood in a dreary kind of silence, sweating beneath the merciless sun. Ash saw, from the drooping smile on Dain's face, that he had not expected the Priestess to place such faith in the girl, in the gods.

The Priestess raised her head and smiled placidly. 'I said earlier that each of the Four Fathers would devise their own trial. The girl is the first, the drought is the second, the death of the sun will be the third.' She looked at Dain as though he were a mosquito, fat with the blood of others. A mosquito she intended to turn into a red smear. 'I think we might just have witnessed the Four Fathers' final test: revolt.'

It was Dain's turn to be scrutinised by the villagers. He shot a nervous look at Tristan, who looked to the sky, as though he expected to be crushed by an invisible hand. But there was nothing there but the sun: the flaming eye that watched, and never blinked.

'No harm will come to the girl,' the Priestess declared.

The villagers looked on – scared, confused, thirsty – and for a moment no one moved. From far below came the mournful sound of a sheep bleating. It seemed to rouse the villagers. There were chores to do, children to admonish, hours to grind out till nightfall.

'Four Fathers be praised!' someone called.

The Priestess bowed her head. 'And may they always guide you.'

The villagers began to drift away. The Priestess looked up and studied the sky.

'Take shelter tonight,' she said. 'There's a storm coming.'

4

As the sun finally fell towards the western hills, a firm breeze whipped the scrubby grass, and a low bank of dark cloud crept up behind the church tower. Down in the village, people cast fearful glances at the sky and covered windows with stout wooden shutters. The air thickened, grew heavy, curled its mighty hands into fists. It fizzed with unspent energy, and it lay upon everything like a rough blanket.

Ash stood at the back door watching the storm build. It would bring rain, but it would also bring ruin. Tonight, the villagers would cower in their homes while the Ancestors stalked between the buildings like giants, thrashing and crushing and ripping the world apart.

The sun was loathsome, but the storms were dreaded above all else.

The Priestess appeared behind Ash. She wore a simple smock, and her pale skin was shiny with sweat. Thin strands of hair clung to her forehead, blood-red in the dying light. She held a small sack in her hand and offered it to Ash. 'For the girl.'

Ash looked from the sack to the church on the next hill, and the menacing sky above it. 'Now?'

'She will be hungry and thirsty.'

'But . . . the storm.'

'If you do not go now, she will be hungry and thirsty until it passes.' She pushed the sack into his hand. The Priestess's fingers were trembling.

'Are you unwell, Priestess?'

She shook her head and smiled, but it was a smile he knew would become a grimace the moment he left.

'It might be the blood sickness,' Ash said, trying not to think of his mother. 'I could fetch Wren from the village.'

'I do not need a healer, Ash. I am not sick. Besides, I have the Ancestors.'

The distant storm grumbled and boomed. Something in the air shifted: the pressure dropped. Little goosebumps rose along Ash's arms.

'Have I been like a mother to you, Ash?'

Ash's head snapped around. He had never heard the Priestess mention his mother before. The only people who mentioned his mother were the children from the village, in their cruellest moments. They were the times he stood and fought, no matter how unfavourable the odds.

He felt the coarse sacking in his fist, felt his heart begin to pound. He couldn't speak. He could never speak when someone mentioned his mother.

'I was blessed with a wise head, but not a warm heart,' the Priestess said. 'I suspect things would have been better for you had I been made a different way.'

Ash said nothing. It felt as though the Priestess was prising the lid off a chest that was crammed full of things he could never put back.

'Life has not been kind to us, but it has treated you worse than most. Your parents were good people. And, as is so often the case, the good people are outlived by the bad.'

Ash looked at the flagstone floor. 'Why are you telling me this?' he asked, through gritted teeth.

The Priestess gripped him by the shoulders and shook him gently. 'You are *good*, Ash. Like them. They would be proud, as I am proud. There is not much goodness left in the world, but there is goodness in you. Do not let anything crush that.'

Ash gasped a breath. 'Why do they do it, Priestess? Why do the Ancestors punish us?' He looked up, his vision thick with tears. 'Do they hate us?'

The Priestess loosened her grip. 'They do not hate us,' she said. 'They punish us because it brings out the best in us, and the worst. It shows us who we are.'

Ash hung his head. A tear, a precious drop of water and salt, hit the ground with a dark splash. 'I am weak,' he said.

'And yet you stand. The important thing to remember is that even when you want it to be over – even when it feels like it must already be over – it is not. As long as you breathe, it goes on. You have power as long as you are alive. Do you understand?'

Ash nodded.

'Good. Now go and feed that poor girl.'

'Yes, Priestess.' He turned and set off into the blustery evening.

'Ash.'

He stopped and looked back. The sun, peeking beneath the seam of thunderclouds, bathed the Priestess in pink light. She looked holy, ethereal.

'Yes, Priestess?'

'My name is Helena.'

He nodded, quite sure that – the two of them aside – only the Ancestors knew her true name.

He turned back to the approaching storm and plunged forwards. It was almost impossible to stay upright: violent gusts buffeted him and the sloping ground seemed to shift beneath his feet. He fell more than once on the way down, and he crawled most of the way up – each sudden squall threatening to prise him up and cast him down. He regained his feet at the broken churchyard wall and entered the cemetery at a stoop.

The stillness of the church was eerie after the violence outside, and the wind howled through gaps in the stone like a tormented ghoul.

Two dozen sheep huddled in the centre of the space, shifting nervously beneath an evil sky. Pewter clouds gathered above, coiling themselves into a seething, ragged vortex. The air pressure dropped further. There wasn't much time.

'Bronwyn,' Ash hissed. He wondered why he was whispering when there was no one nearby, and the wind was loud enough to drown the sheep's bleating.

He stepped towards the room at the end of the church, where he had told her to hide. He hadn't gone more than three steps when a shadow detached itself from one of the statues and turned to face him. Ash nearly dropped the sack.

'Did I scare you?' Bronwyn asked. In the gloom, her black eye looked like a hole in her head.

Ash cleared his throat. 'No. Of course not.' He held out the sack. 'Here. I brought you something.'

Bronwyn snatched it and withdrew a waterskin. She tipped her head back and took a greedy gulp.

'Don't drink it all at once,' Ash said. 'I don't know when I'll be able to come back.' He thought of the shrinking pool. 'Or whether there will be any water left this time tomorrow.'

High above, the air cracked like a great whip. White light streaked across the seething sky.

'I have to go back,' Ash said. 'I'll return when I can.' He moved to the doorway and hesitated. The wind whipped around the tombstones and howled beneath the archway. He could see the House on the Hill across the valley, could almost feel its sturdy safety. He had to get back, but he knew the wind would fight him from all angles. He stepped outside.

'Stop!' Bronwyn shouted, pulling Ash violently back as a brilliant bolt flashed across the sky and struck the church's weathervane. It erupted in a splash of sparks, sending a cascade of masonry over the entrance to the church.

Ash stared at the place he would have been had Bronwyn not pulled him back – it was now just a jumble of timber and tiles and stone. Behind him, sheep barged into one another – wide-eyed and fearful – bleating as they fought to find the centre of the flock. Ash drew a deep, shaky breath and tasted the scent of something scorched, like bones in a fire. He shivered.

She saved my life.

He opened his mouth, but for some reason could not give voice to the thought. He shrugged Bronwyn's hand from his arm.

'There's no need to thank me,' Bronwyn said, retracting her hand as though scalded.

'You almost got me killed.'

'What?'

'I only came out during the storm because of you.' He looked at the wild weather. The rain had begun to lash down. 'And now I'm stranded here.'

'I just saved your life!'

Ash knew it was true, but he still could not admit it to this stranger – this *outsider*. He finally turned to face her. 'And I saved yours – twice! What do you think the villagers would have done to you if I hadn't brought you here? How much longer do you think you'd have lasted if I hadn't brought food and water? As far as I'm concerned, we're not even close to being even.'

Bronwyn made a noise of disgust and moved to sit against the opposite wall. Ash watched the storm rage outside, hoping that it would pass as quickly as it had come. But the Ancestors were clearly furious about something, and the longer it raged the more convinced he became that that something was the girl.

It only occurred to him late in the night, moments before falling asleep, that it might be him.

5

Ash woke to find a column of sheep passing before him, picking their way over the pile of debris and out into the valley to graze.

Bronwyn was nowhere to be seen.

He got up, his shirt sticking to his back, and walked outside. The morning was warm and damp. The violence of the storm had been replaced by an eerie, heavy stillness that was only broken by an occasional bleat from below. He didn't expect to find Bronwyn – he was half hoping she had solved the village's problem by taking herself off – but she was there, just beyond the crumbling churchyard wall, at the point where the hill dropped into the valley.

He walked over to her, his body stiff with sleep. He passed the maimed statue, now face down in the sickly grass, and came to a stop beside Bronwyn. He yawned.

'Is it normally this quiet after a storm?' she asked.

Ash looked down at the scattering of grey buildings below. It was odd. No one was out inspecting the damage. No one was out gossiping. No one was gazing at the cloud-shredded sky, whispering thanks to the Ancestors for their mercy. The village was perfectly still, and the expression on Bronwyn's face unsettled Ash just as much as the peculiar tranquillity. It was, in a strange way, like being underwater.

'This is what happened in your village, isn't it?' he asked.

Bronwyn gazed into the valley. She seemed desperate to find one of the people who hated her – someone who would prove that she was not the curse she seemed to be.

Eventually, unable to speak, she nodded.

Ash scanned the village. Nothing. No one. Not a sound besides the mournful moaning of sheep. His chest filled with a queasy unrest. The prospect of every person he had ever known vanishing overnight filled him with a confusion of feelings. He had wished for this very outcome on more occasions than he could count, so there was relief, and yet they were still *his* people, and not all of them had been unkind. Mildred, the slaughterman's wife, had furtively given him a dripping heap of offal once. 'For *you*,' she'd whispered. 'Not your mistress.' And then there was Quinn, who had stepped in when Ash found himself cornered by three of the older boys. 'If I see one of them after you,' he'd said, 'I'll leave him to it. But there's no honour in three against one. I can't stand by while that happens.'

They had both known his parents, so perhaps not everyone believed the stories about his father.

He turned his eyes to the House on the Hill. It stood there, somehow quieter and meeker than he had ever known it to be. He sensed there was something he was not seeing – something in his line of vision that his eyes or his brain or his heart refused to witness.

Bronwyn saw it first, and whatever it was made her gasp.

Slowly, Ash's eyes fell to the pool at the foot of the valley. It was low despite the night's torrential rainfall. Dangerously low: a puddle in a rocky crater. But that was not what made the blood drain from his face.

As he looked – as his eyes finally began to *see* – the sun burned through a tattered flag of cloud and picked out something in the water. Something that shone like a rare metal: a halo of burnished copper.

He was racing down the hill before he knew his feet

had moved. He flew at dangerous speed, his lungs full of dread, his eyes fixed on the pool. Within seconds he was no longer high enough to see what lay at the bottom, but that only increased his fear. He ran faster, missed his footing, tumbled, bounced, rolled. Flinty rocks concealed in the grass tore little chunks from his body, gouging wounds he wouldn't feel till much later. He picked himself up and ran until the slope began to level out.

He came to the lip of the crater and saw up close what his eyes had refused to see from afar. A simple, pale gown, clinging to a still body. A fan of red hair, soft and sheeny above the waterline, blood-red at the sodden tips.

She lay face down.

The water around her was completely still.

Ash scurried down the rocky slope, slipping on smooth pebbles that had only ever felt cool beneath his soles but were now baked to burning. He splashed into the water, braced for the ground to fall away as the pool dropped to its bottomless depths, but he reached the middle without even wetting his shirt.

He grabbed the Priestess – *Helena*, he thought, *her name is Helena* – and dragged her towards the edge, ignoring how heavy she felt, ignoring the coolness of her skin beneath his fingers. As soon as she was clear of the water, the weight and awkwardness of her body began to sap his strength. He threaded his hands beneath her armpits and hauled her backwards. He slipped, squirmed in agony as a rock rolled against his spine, got up again. Helena's head rested heavily on her chest.

'Come on!' he said, heaving again, falling again. 'Four Fathers, please!'

He tried once more and fell heavily on the small of his back. He winced against the pain. 'Help me!' Tears streamed across his cheeks. *To cry is a crime*. All that water wasted. He rested his head against Helena's. 'Help me.'

A small scurry of rocks bounced past him and landed in the pool with a *plop*. Bronwyn was beside him. 'Don't touch her!' Ash shouted, clutching Helena's body closer to him. 'You did this!'

Bronwyn backed up the rocky slope, leaving a careful distance between them. 'I didn't do this,' she said, quietly.

Ash scrunched his eyes shut and pushed his face deeper into Helena's hair. A sound of anguish escaped from between his gritted teeth. Bronwyn edged closer and lifted a hand. She held it over his shoulder for a few moments before letting it fall. Ash flinched as her fingers touched him, but he did not shrug them away.

'What is happening to us?' he asked, his voice muffled. 'Why have the Four Fathers forsaken us?'

Bronwyn opened her mouth but closed it without speaking. She squeezed Ash's shoulder. They sat like that for a long time, until the sun had risen high enough to peek over the edge of the crater.

Its burning touch seemed to stir Ash. It was the first physical sensation he'd felt since Bronwyn reached out to comfort him. Her hand was still there, but it had long since become weightless. He lifted his head, and Bronwyn finally withdrew her hand.

'Let me help you,' she said, gently. 'We can't leave her down here.'

Ash nodded slowly. He eased himself up, being careful not to disturb Helena's body, and felt all the little bruises and scratches and bloody nicks in his flesh for the first time.

'We'll take it slowly,' Bronwyn said. 'One step at a time.'

They laid Helena down carefully, and Ash was able to look at her properly for the first time. Her eyes were closed, and her face had settled into the serene expression she wore while stream-dreaming. Her gown and hair had dried in the time it had taken them to carry her out of the crater, and were it not for the pallor of her skin, the blue tinge to her lips, the stillness of her chest, she might have been sleeping.

Ash looked up to the House on the Hill. Bronwyn followed his gaze and seemed to read his mind.

'We will,' she said, still breathing hard, 'but first we rest.'

They sat with their legs dangling over the lip of the crater, staring at the dwindling puddle of water at the bottom. By sunset it would be gone: an unchanging feature of Ash's childhood lost to the air.

'We're in trouble,' Ash said. It didn't need to be said – what with the sun resting on their faces like a slap – but he said it all the same. He looked up, to the south, where there was nothing but rocky rubble. He wondered how long it would take for the entire valley to look the same.

'Does the village have a store of water anywhere else?' Bronwyn asked.

'There's a tub in the House on the Hill, but that's it. Everyone scoops what they need from the stream each morning. We mustn't take more than we need, lest we anger the Four Fathers.'

Bronwyn looked over her shoulder, towards the silent village. 'We can't stay here. We'll die of thirst.'

'I know.'

'But where can we go?'

'There's nothing to the south,' Ash said.

'So we go north?'

Ash nodded, grimly. 'That's where the water came from.'

'It's where I came from, too. There's no one in the next two villages. What if the same . . . curse has fallen everywhere?'

'Then it's just you and me.' Ash tossed a stone into the puddle far below. 'Let's hope that isn't the case.'

Bronwyn turned her bruised face towards him. Her right eye narrowed; the other was already swollen shut. 'You do realise that – so far as we know – we're the only people left? You might want to start treating me like someone who could help you. Someone who *has* helped you.'

Ash shot her a sideways look but said nothing.

'Do you really think I'm cursed? That I somehow made fifty people disappear?'

'Do you have another explanation?'

'No, I don't. But that doesn't mean there isn't one.'

They fell silent, and the silence was absolute. Ash couldn't look at Bronwyn without wondering why the Four Fathers had sent her, and why he had been the only one left behind. More than anything, he wanted to know why they hadn't protected Helena, when for so long she had dedicated her life to them.

But to question the Four Fathers was blasphemy. He pinched himself on the thigh as a small act of penance.

'We should go,' he said, wincing as he got to his feet. 'The sooner we leave, the better our chances of finding more water.'

Bronwyn went with him to Helena, and together they carried her up the hill. The morning was hot now, and their hair hung in sweaty, straggly strands by the time they reached the back door. Only last night Ash had stood there while Helena apologised for failings that never were. Looking back now, it almost seemed as though she had been saying goodbye.

And then it struck him.

Helena had known. She had known some terrible vengeance would take the villagers. And for some reason she had sent Ash to the church, putting him out of harm's way, when she could have gone and saved herself. But why? There was no way to know for certain – the ways of the Ancestors were strange – but he looked upon the Priestess with new curiosity, and a new love.

He silently scolded himself. Loving, like crying, was a waste. More than that, it was a curse. Everyone he'd ever loved had ended up like this: Helena, his mother, his father. He hadn't seen his father's body, of course, and even now he clung to the hope that he might still be alive somewhere. He reprimanded himself again. His father had gone out into the wilderness. He was dead. *A sheep that shuns the flock is a sheep that feeds the dogs.* Ash shook his head firmly. Hope was foolish, worse than love. Nobody survived beyond the boundary.

And yet, very soon now, that is where he and his strange companion would have to go. *North.* The thought sent a shiver from his neck to his heels.

'Where?' Bronwyn asked, gasping for breath.

'Upstairs,' Ash said.

Bronwyn nodded, and he almost thanked her for not protesting at the final effort. Almost.

They struggled up the stairs. The room was dark and cool: the shutters still drawn against the storm. They laid the Priestess of Last Village on her bed. Ash folded her

hands across her stomach, bowed his head, and prayed
to the Four Fathers to keep her in their care.

For ever and ever. Amen.

6

The village was silent. Some doors were open and others were shut. Fallen roof tiles lay shattered in the street, and shutters hung from hinges on every other house.

'Empty,' Bronwyn said, as she peered in through a darkened window. 'They're all gone.'

Ash stepped out of a house on the other side of the street, a bloated waterskin slung across his body. Despite all appearances, he had expected to find someone – maybe even everyone – hiding in some unknown shelter.

'What happened here?' Bronwyn asked.

Ash looked at the squat stone houses surrounding him. The destruction wrought by the storm made it impossible to tell whether the villagers had been dragged from their homes or whether they'd left of their own accord. He said as much to Bronwyn.

'How many people would it take to abduct an entire village?'

Ash shrugged. 'A lot. But I suppose nobody would know it was happening while the storm was raging, and the watchers wouldn't be able to raise the alarm. A small group might have gone from house to house.'

Bronwyn shook her head. 'Where would they have come from? I didn't see anyone for miles when I left my village.'

Ash didn't have an answer to that. 'What did your village look like after everyone disappeared?'

Bronwyn dropped her gaze to the ground. 'My village isn't much like this one.'

'How is it different?'

'We live – *lived* – apart. It's hard to explain.' She shook her head in irritation. 'It doesn't matter. Everyone was just gone. There wasn't anything to suggest they'd been taken. Anyway, why would anyone even want to abduct an entire village? It doesn't make any sense.'

Ash nudged a fragment of roof tile absentmindedly with his foot. 'If they weren't taken, they must have left. But where would they go?'

They both turned their heads to look along the winding street: northwards. Hills rose at the end of the village, their grass bleached in the midday sun. Beyond them, a jagged shadow against the sky, were the

Nameless Mountains. And beyond those . . .

'The Kingdom,' Ash whispered. 'Do you think the Four Fathers finally called them home?' His face was pale and stricken. 'Do you think we missed the salvation?'

Bronwyn frowned. 'What are you talking about? What's the Kingdom?'

Ash took an involuntary step away from Bronwyn. 'You've never heard of the Kingdom?'

Bronwyn shook her head. For a moment, Ash couldn't speak. He had never encountered such heathenish ignorance before. Even the toddlers of Last Village knew about the Kingdom.

Bronwyn folded her arms across her chest. 'Are you going to tell me what it is or not?'

Slowly, Ash found his voice. He whispered a quick prayer to the Ancestors. 'The Kingdom is a sacred place – a holy place – where people go when they die. There are vast lakes of pure water, feasts every day, and more plants and animals than you could possibly imagine.'

Bronwyn raised a single eyebrow and kept her arms crossed.

'What?' Ash said. 'It's true. There are pictures of the animals in Helena's books. I've seen them!'

'And I suppose there are no storms in this place, and

the sun is meek, and everybody holds hands and nobody ever fights?'

Ash's face brightened. 'So you have heard of it?'

Bronwyn rolled her eyes. 'No. I'm just guessing what this fairytale place you've been tricked into believing might be like.'

'It's not a trick. It's real.'

'But if you only go there when you die, how do you know? How can anyone know?'

Ash pressed his lips into a thin line. 'Helena communes with the Ancestors, and *they* know. Besides, plenty of people think it's a place here on Earth – far to the north – but you can't get there if you go looking for it. You have to be summoned by the Four Fathers.'

'Well, isn't that convenient.'

Ash scowled. 'Not if you get left behind with a heathen.'

There was moment of tense silence. The sun beat down. Rafters squeaked and groaned in the heat.

Bronwyn unfolded her arms and placed her hands on her hips. 'So how do you explain what happened in my village? We don't believe our forefathers will save us.'

Ash shot Bronwyn a glance that could have cut slate. 'That's blasphemy.'

Bronwyn shrugged. 'It's true. We don't believe they're

listening, or that one day they'll come to save us.'

'It doesn't matter if you believe it or not: it's still true.'

'But it doesn't make sense! Our ancestors are dead, and the dead don't come back.'

'That's enough!' Ash inhaled deeply. The air was so warm it was like breathing someone else's breath.

Bronwyn glanced at the House on the Hill. 'Sorry. I shouldn't have said that about the dead.'

'No. You shouldn't have. The Four Fathers see and hear everything.' Ash took another breath. 'But you're right. It doesn't explain what happened to Helena. She devoted her life to the Ancestors. There's no way they would leave her behind – leave her like that.'

The pair stood in silence, on opposite sides of the narrow street. When Bronwyn finally spoke her voice was low. 'What do you think happened to her?'

Ash had been trying to avoid asking himself that very question, and yet his mind kept returning to it, like a mosquito returning to a slumbering body, over and over again. It was not impossible that she had sacrificed herself, but Ash could not think of that without a crushing sense of guilt.

She wouldn't do that, not unless . . . Unless it was what the Ancestors demanded of her. Perhaps Dain was right.

Perhaps the Four Fathers needed blood, and Helena's sacrifice spared the rest of us.

Her final words now seemed to be full of clues and warnings he had been too preoccupied with the coming storm to heed.

The good people are outlived by the bad.

'I don't know,' he said eventually, truthfully. He hung his head, and the sun fell on his hair like a molten crown. 'We need to go.'

'But where?'

Ash glared at Bronwyn through dark strands of hair. 'The Kingdom.' Bronwyn opened her mouth but Ash cut her off. 'I know you don't believe it exists but we have to go north anyway, so we'll soon find out.' He swept his hair away from his face. 'You search the houses on that side for provisions. I'll take this side.'

He stepped through an open doorway without another word, and they slowly made their way through the village, searching cupboards and shelves for anything edible. They did not find much – a few dried herbs, some shrivelled berries, strips of cured mutton – but they found enough to know the residents had not been prepared for a long journey.

In a low house that reeked of blood, Ash found the

club that Kelly used to stun sheep. The discovery made him even more certain that the villagers had been summoned to the Kingdom. After all, only one of the Four Fathers could persuade Kelly to part with his beloved club, and the Kingdom was a place where such cruel weapons had no purpose. Kelly had surrendered it with every other symbol of their suffering.

The thought of being left behind terrified and exhilarated Ash in equal measure. On the one hand, he feared that the gates to the Kingdom would be closed by the time they reached it, and he would be left to wander the world for ever. On the other, he was witnessing the thing that had been promised for generations: deliverance. An end to his misery was in sight.

Ash turned the club over in his hands, then tucked it beneath the cord around his waist.

At the end of the village, Ash and Bronwyn put their plunder into two satchels and slung them across their chests. Except for the waterskin that Ash had filled from the tub in the House on the Hill, they travelled with no more than the clothes on their backs.

'Are you ready?' Ash said.

Bronwyn looked up at the hills looming before them. 'No.'

'Me neither, but we don't have much choice.'

Ash adjusted the strap on his shoulder and stepped into the dry streambed. The stones already looked as though water was a distant memory: little puffs of dust rose up between their feet, and the dry clacking sound they made was a far cry from the babbling rush of water.

They made steady, if meandering, progress between the hills. Clouds of mosquitoes swirled around Ash's head. He tried to swat them whenever they landed on his skin but soon gave up. Bronwyn didn't seem to notice them: she just plodded steadily on. They did not talk. It was only when they came to what had been a small waterfall, and they were forced to climb into the surrounding hills, that they spoke again. Ash stopped when he reached a lonely hut – the Northern Post – and looked back at the village far below.

'What is it?' Bronwyn asked.

'This is the furthest I've ever been,' Ash said.

'You mean you haven't left the village before?'

'No. Never.'

Bronwyn surveyed the view. 'You can still see the House on the Hill from here.' She pointed at a grey square atop a distant hill.

'That's why I haven't been any further,' Ash said. 'This is the last place we know to be safe.' He gave a short, bitter laugh, and Bronwyn cast a questioning look at him.

'What's funny?'

'Nothing,' Ash said. 'I just realised that for years I've been known as the son of a deserter, and here I am: the last person to leave Last Village.'

Bronwyn seemed on the cusp of asking something, but then Ash turned away, and the question went unspoken.

They both looked to the north. Scraggy plants cowered in the shelter of grey rocks, mighty trees lay uprooted, and rolling hills morphed into jagged mountains.

'What's it like out there?' Ash said.

Bronwyn swallowed and wiped a bead of sweat from her temple. 'Wild.' She looked across at Ash. 'You might want to use some bloodweed; you're making the mozzies fat.'

Ash reached into his bag of provisions and took out a bouquet of dark red leaves. He tore one away from the bunch and began rubbing it over himself; the sap left pinkish smears and an acrid smell on his skin, but it drove the mosquitoes away.

They went on: downhill and uphill and downhill again. The way became overgrown with weeds and nettles and long grasses that plucked at their clothes. An intermittent wall along an ancient roadway had suppressed some of the growth, but they were frequently forced to clamber over piles of broken stone. Sweat dripped from their noses, and when they reached the top of the third hill they stopped to drink from the waterskin.

'One mouthful,' Bronwyn said, 'every two hours.'

Ash nodded and lifted the spout to his parched mouth. The water tasted sweet and fresh, and it soothed his throat as he swallowed it. He passed the waterskin to Bronwyn, who filled her mouth but didn't swallow immediately. Ash wished he had done the same; his mouth already felt sticky and sandy. He stoppered the skin and slung it back across his chest. 'Shall we eat something?' he said, peering hopefully into his bag.

Bronwyn shook her head: her cheeks were still swollen with water.

'Why not?'

Bronwyn rolled her eyes and swallowed. 'You should only eat when you feel hungry.'

'I do feel hungry. I didn't have breakfast.'

'No, I mean really hungry. When it feels like your stomach is eating itself.'

Ash looked down into the bag. Reluctantly, he closed it.

'We're going to be hungry a lot,' Bronwyn said, 'but hungry is better than starving.' She saw that her words hadn't done much to cheer Ash. 'We'll eat something when we get past Deddon, okay?'

Ash nodded. 'How far is it?'

'Not far,' Bronwyn said.

They staggered down a steep gully and clambered up the other side. The ridge of the hill curved north so they walked along its spine, looking down into the valleys on either side. They didn't see a soul. In the distance, they glimpsed a long, dusty plain.

'That used to be Lake Wendy,' Bronwyn said. 'Largest lake in the land, supposedly.'

It was hard to imagine a lake there. It looked like a wound that had shrunk to a thin scar of dust.

'What happened?' Ash said.

They stopped at the hump of the hill, to take one last look at Lake Wendy before they began their descent.

'The sun.'

The dry lakebed troubled Ash, and he struggled to

ignore it. It was only when Bronwyn tugged at his sleeve and pointed to the other side of the ridge that he turned away.

'There,' Bronwyn said. 'Deddon.'

Ash had rarely imagined what other villages might look like, and whenever he had he always assumed they would resemble his own, so what lay before him was a surprise. A dozen or so huts were scattered across the hillside. There did not seem to be any pattern to the way they had been built: each was clearly made from whatever had been lying around at the time. The only thing each shack had in common was that there was nothing else around it. The huts were spaced so far apart that it would have been a stretch to describe their residents as neighbours, or the entirety of them as a village.

'Nobody trusted anybody,' Bronwyn said. 'We didn't share. The only rule was that you looked after yourself.'

'Do you want to go back there?'

'What for? It's deserted, and it's not like I have anything to go back for.'

It was Ash's turn to hesitate on the brink of asking a question. He knew so little about her, and what he did know was based on rumour and assumption. Bronwyn seemed to sense the impending question and hunched her shoulders against it.

'We have to keep going,' she said. 'Through there.'

Ash followed Bronwyn's gaze along the spine of the ridge. There was another settlement – the dead feel of it palpable even at this distance – and beyond that lay a dark mass. It stained the landscape like the shadow of a thundercloud, but the sky was blue.

'What is that?' Ash said.

Bronwyn had already set off. She did not look back. 'The Burned Forest,' she said.

7

The ground was soft and mulchy underfoot. The air smelled of smoke. Nothing moved in the blackened landscape except for Ash and Bronwyn.

There was no path and no way of knowing how vast the forest might be. The sight of so much death and decay made Ash long for some sign of life, but it was a place of ghosts. He could feel it. He did not need to know the history of the place to know something terrible had happened here. He pushed the thought away, and tried to focus on something other than the tickly thirst in his throat.

Even though there were no leaves on the trees, they seemed to cast an all-encompassing shadow. It was impossible to see any distance into the woods. The place was eerie and deathly quiet, empty in a way that left it full of something else – something sinister.

Bronwyn stopped to touch a blistered trunk, and a

dark chunk of bark fell into her palm. 'Do you know what happened here?' she said.

Ash turned on the spot, looking up at the blue sky between shattered shards of trees.

'There was a fire,' he said.

Something hit him on the side of head. He flinched and let out a startled shout. When he turned, he found Bronwyn dusting soot from her fingertips.

'What was that for?' Ash said, rubbing his temple.

'*There was a fire*,' she said. She held her hands out wide. 'Enlighten me further, oh wise one.'

'How am I supposed to know?'

'Don't your gods give you any answers?'

'No,' Ash said. 'They speak to Helena, not me.' He paused. 'Spoke.'

Bronwyn looked as though she wanted to say more, but instead she walked away, kicking clumps of mulch that turned the toes of her sheepskin boots black. Ash strode after her.

'Are you trying to say that Helena wasn't in communion with the Ancestors? She knew things that everyone else has forgotten.'

Bronwyn stopped. 'If everyone else has forgotten, how can anyone know if they're true? How do you know the Ancestors are even there?'

Ash pursed his lips. He had never heard anyone blaspheme so openly before. There were laws against it. But, although he could never admit it to Bronwyn, the thought had crossed his mind too. What other explanation could there be for such a life as his? He pushed the doubts away and told himself that his sorry life was punishment for his lack of faith. But still, the thoughts remained, just waiting for him to grow curious or desperate enough to study them.

'You should keep your thoughts to yourself – especially if we're travelling together. I don't want to be nearby when the Four Fathers strike you down.'

'Why should I? If they *do* exist then we must be the butt of all their jokes. Look around you.' She stepped backwards, sweeping an arm to indicate the dead forest. 'What could they possibly do to us that's worse than this?'

Ash opened his mouth, but the words were yanked from his throat. He watched as the ground opened up and swallowed Bronwyn whole. The earth around her stirred into life: bark and branches were pulled into the void. Ash tried to scramble away but the ground beneath his feet moved too, knocking him down and dragging him backwards, towards the rim.

He made one final, desperate lunge, grabbing a handful of slimy, rotten mulch, but it was futile. He slid over the edge and into darkness.

Ash expected to fall and keep falling, to tumble endlessly in a black emptiness. But it was just a hole – a pit – and Bronwyn broke his fall.

'Ow!' she said, rolling away from him.

Ash grunted. 'Serves you right,' he said, getting to his feet. 'You brought this on us. I told you not to insult the Four Fathers.'

Bronwyn stood up and looked around the hole. A pool of brown water lay in the bottom of it. Rough, muddy walls stretched up on all sides, and a coarse net clung to protruding rocks near the bottom, its middle sagging beneath the waterline of the pool.

'Do your gods dig many holes?' she said. 'This is a trap.'

Ash took in his surroundings for the first time. The pit had clearly been dug by people: there were rough marks on the walls where the earth had been scraped out. It was not the work of the Ancestors, that was for sure. They dealt in droughts and diseases, not mud and toil. Ash unhooked the edge of the net from where it had snagged on a nearby rock and let it drop into the pool with a splash.

'Who made it, do you think?' he said.

Bronwyn shrugged, perching on a thick root that emerged from the wall to form a kind of seat. 'I don't know. I suppose we'll either find out or we won't.'

'What do you mean?'

Bronwyn gazed up at the circle of sky far above. 'Well, either whoever set the trap will come for us before our supplies run out, or they won't.'

A nasty shiver of panic crawled over Ash's skin. 'Maybe we could climb out?' he said, but already his eyes were travelling up the sheer sides of the pit, taking in the higher places where helpful roots had been cut close to the wall.

'Did you do much climbing as a priestess's servant?' Bronwyn asked.

Ash felt too sick to respond. He had known, deep down, that he would fail to reach the Kingdom. There was a reason he had been left behind, after all. But he had expected his quest to last longer than a day. There were children in the village who claimed to have come this far just on a dare.

He thought of whoever had dug the hole, and realised

that they must be many. A village, perhaps. It would take days to move such a large amount of earth. And if there were many of them, they probably checked the hole regularly; no one ate so well as to leave a trap unchecked for long. Then again, maybe the pit had been dug years ago and had lain undisturbed ever since, its excavators moved on or dead. He couldn't decide which would be worse: to dwell in the hole until their supplies ran out, or to be hauled from it by people who were too hungry to care that their trap had caught something other than lost sheep.

It happened, apparently, out there. *Cannibalism.* Villagers told stories about it to frighten the children, to keep them from straying too far from safety. Helena never wanted to talk about it, which made Ash think the stories were probably true.

Only it's not out there *any more*, Ash thought. *It's out* here.

He waded through the water and sat on a swollen root, on the opposite side of the pit to Bronwyn. He swung his bag of supplies around his body and set it on his knees. He expected Bronwyn to object when he took out a strip of cured mutton, but she only held out a hand for one of her own.

'Just one each,' she said.

Ash nodded. He understood what she wasn't saying: they might be stuck in the pit for some time. He tossed a piece across. The meat was chewy and salty and tasted slightly of muddy water, but it felt good to be eating something. Ash tore off great chunks and forced them down, whereas Bronwyn nibbled at the corners, making each bite last as long as possible. It meant that Ash had to spend a long time watching Bronwyn eat, wishing he had made his own portion last longer.

They soon came to loathe the pit. It was a miserable place. The only redeeming feature was that, compared to the sun-baked world above, it was refreshingly cool. But their feet felt soft and numb inside their soaking boots, and the sun wouldn't pass over the pit's opening until the following noon. If another storm struck in the meantime – a particularly bad one – they'd have another problem.

'Can you swim?' Ash said.

Bronwyn seemed to know why he was asking. She looked at the sky and shook her head. Ash wasn't surprised. Most people couldn't swim. It was a useless skill in a drought-stricken world.

As they sat in silence, a rat emerged from a dark nook

and climbed on top of a rock. It held out its front paws, twitched its whiskers, and then scrambled up the wall. They watched it ascend higher and higher, its small claws clinging to the narrowest of crevices, until it finally reached the top and dragged itself over the rim. Bronwyn put her chin in her hands and sighed.

'There goes dinner,' she said.

Ash scowled. He peered up at the lip of the hole, hoping that the rat might poke its face back inside, but obviously it had gone off to do whatever it was rats went off to do.

Ash found himself staring at the darkening sky. The fading light seemed to sink them deeper in the hole. They sat in silence. Each kept to their own side of the pit, trying to decide how to feel about the other. It was like one of those ancient strategy games played with pieces of bone on a chequered board, only their pieces were made of silence, and their board was made of time.

And it was a game neither of them could win.

8

Night came early to the pit. The circle of sky overhead was still a shade of blue, but it darkened steadily. The pool at the bottom shone glossy and black.

'How are your feet?' Ash said. It was the first thing he had said for some time, and in truth he was asking to reassure himself more than anything else. He could no longer see Bronwyn on the opposite side of the pit.

He heard sloshing, followed by a trickle.

'Wet,' Bronwyn said. 'Yours?'

'Wet. Wet and cold.'

'Probably something to do with all this water . . .'

'Ha,' Ash said, without humour. 'Shall we have another mutton chew?'

'No. We shouldn't eat if we're not moving.'

Ash's heart sank. 'A swig of water, then?'

'Not from the waterskin. Try the puddle if you're thirsty.'

'Let me guess: because we're not moving?'

'Exactly. You'll thank me when we're trekking in the heat again.'

'We have to get out of here first.'

'I know. We will.'

Ash had no patience for Bronwyn's newfound optimism. She sounded much too cheerful for someone who had spent hours stuck in a waterlogged hole. It only added to his misery.

'What makes you think we'll get out?'

'There's no point expecting to stay in here for ever. We'll never escape with that attitude.'

'How can you be so optimistic?' he asked.

'You're being optimistic too.'

Bronwyn couldn't see it, but Ash's face had been crumpled in a permanent frown for the past hour. 'What makes you say that?'

'If you thought our situation was really hopeless you'd have eaten all your food by now. But you haven't, and it's because you know there's a future to save it for.'

Ash was tempted to stuff his mouth full of food, just to prove Bronwyn wrong, but he didn't. Annoyingly, he found it hard to argue with her logic.

'It's a good thing you've got me with you,' Bronwyn said. 'Don't you think?'

Ash opened his mouth and rejected the first thing that arrived on his tongue. The second wasn't any more polite. He settled for the third – something his mother used to say to him whenever he ran an errand for her as a small boy.

'I'd be lost without you.'

He did his best to make it sound like a genuine sentiment – it was certainly true enough – and, after a moment's pause, Bronwyn accepted it as such.

'It's nothing. You'll be lost *with* me when we finally get out of this forest.'

Something suddenly dropped on to Ash's shoulder. It gave him such a fright that his legs shot out, churning the still pool into choppy, frothy confusion. He yelped.

'What is it?' Bronwyn asked. Already she was wading across the pool. 'What happened?'

The panic in Ash's chest subsided, but his heart kept pounding. 'Nothing,' he said. 'I'm fine. It was just that rat.'

He heard Bronwyn huff and mutter as she splashed back across the pool. The rat – wherever it had run to – was squeaking insistently.

'It sounds hurt,' she said. 'Hurt or frightened.'

Bronwyn's words jolted Ash upright. It felt as though he had fallen into another, much deeper, pit.

Hurt. Frightened.

'Someone's coming,' he said.

Adrenaline coursed through Ash's veins but there was nothing he could do and nowhere for him to go. He felt the true helplessness of the trap. He was paralysed by fear – fear of whatever approached through the black mulch above.

Wordlessly, they both moved into the centre of the pool. They stood side by side and looked up at the indigo sky.

Soil and stones fell into the pit, dislodged by the weight of whatever approached, landing in the water with a soft patter. Seconds passed that felt like hours. Ash and Bronwyn panted, as though competing for the last few breaths available in their sunken cell.

The shower of debris came to an abrupt halt. A head appeared in silhouette over one side of the rim.

'What tasty morsels do we have in here then?' a voice said.

It was not nearly as terrifying a voice as Ash had expected to hear. Perhaps it was the pit and the distance that made it sound so feeble? Then again, it didn't really matter how strong the voice was: it came from outside the trap, and that was power enough.

Ash knew his own voice would sound similarly shaky, but that owed nothing to the acoustics of the hole.

'We're armed,' he said, 'and we're not afraid to fight.'

'Don't say that,' Bronwyn hissed, hitting him on the arm.

'People!' the voice at the top squawked. It sounded like it belonged to a woman. 'Bother. Can't eat those. Well, could. But won't. Not there yet. And if they're armed, hardly worth the trouble of hoisting them out. Have to leave them till weapons won't do them no good. People. Bother! What are the chances?'

'Wait!' Bronwyn called. 'Please don't leave us down here.'

The shape of the woman disappeared. Then it popped back – just a head and shoulders. 'How many are you?'

'Just two,' Bronwyn said.

'Any sheep?'

'No, but we've got some mutton.'

'Even better. I'll just hoist you out then, shall I?'

'Yes, please,' said Ash.

'And you'll feed me up like a queen's cat?'

Ash was momentarily confused. He didn't know what a queen or a cat was. It sounded like a riddle, but the meaning felt clear and safe enough to hazard a reply. 'Yes,' he said. 'We'll share what we have.'

'Right. And at what point do you plan to murder me with those nasty weapons of yours?' (Bronwyn jabbed Ash in the ribs. 'Idiot,' she muttered.) 'Before you feed me, I'll bet! And I'll bet another thing, too. I'll bet that hole started looking like a grave a while ago now. Next thing, you'll be needing someone to put in it. That's what graves are for.'

'No,' Bronwyn said. 'We won't. I promise.'

'You promise? That is very generous of you. I've heard many promises in my time. Fragile things, promises. Easy to break, especially when you swear not to.'

'Please,' Ash said.

'Very polite, you two, for murderers.'

'Please,' Ash said again. He felt close to tears: negotiating with their captor was like trying to swat a mosquito: she didn't stay in one place for long enough. 'Please just let us out.' He swallowed his pride. 'We're only children.'

'Children?' the woman asked. 'People are still having children, are they? Folk are weirder than fungus, you know.' She reached up a hand to scratch her head. 'Children, you say? Honestly?'

'Honestly,' Bronwyn said.

'Hmmm. Well, children is different, I suppose. Children never was the problem. It was always the grown ones. Children were like lambs, lambs to the slaughter.' She suddenly fell silent. 'And you say you've got mutton?'

'*Yes!*' Ash and Bronwyn's voices rang out in unison.

'All right,' she said. 'I'll pull you out. Not fat ones, are you? No, course not. Don't get fat ones any more. Not enough food, not any more.'

Ash's body slumped with relief.

'I'll pull you out as soon as you've proven you're little lambs and not big bad wolfies.'

Ash's shoulders slumped a little further. 'How do we do that?' he asked.

'Simple! Just wait there and I'll come back when it's light. Should be easy enough to tell, even with these old peepers of mine.'

Her head began to disappear again, but Ash was struck by a sudden idea. 'Wait!'

The woman stopped moving. 'What now?'

'How do you know about wolves?'

'Wolfies? Same way I know everything I know. I heard it or saw it or read it. Don't remember which.'

'You can read?'

'Probably. Not done it for a long time now.' She seemed to have a sudden recollection. 'Never met a wolf. No wolfies even in the Olden Days. Anyway, why are you so keen on wolfies? Not common for lambs to be keen on wolfies. Much more common for wolfies to be keen on lambs.'

'Because I've only ever met one person who knew about them: the Priestess in my village, Helena.' Ash paused, fighting hard to resist the urge to keep talking. The woman might disappear at any moment, but he wanted her to hear the Priestess's name. To remember it, maybe. Helena had roamed in her younger years, collecting herbs and roots, scraps of bark and wisdom. She might have come here. Maybe.

Long seconds of silence dripped into the hole. And then: 'You know Helena?'

Ash heard Bronwyn release a long, slow breath.

'I live with her. *Lived* with her.'

'So you're an apprentice priest?' the woman asked.

'No.' Ash lowered his head, swallowed, looked up again. 'A servant.'

'Can't say I'm surprised. Priests are supposed to be wise. Not very wise falling into a hole, is it?'

'I know.'

The woman sighed heavily. 'Does Helena live still?'

'No. She is with the Ancestors now.'

'Ancestors be damned! If I had the Ancestors here I'd throw them in this hole and fill it in before you could say "Amen".'

Bronwyn snorted. Ash suspected that she was growing to quite like the person at the top of the hole, despite everything.

'I'm sorry to hear that Helena is gone,' said the voice. 'Can't say I'm surprised. I seem to outlive everyone I meet.'

Again, Ash remembered Helena's words: *The good people are outlived by the bad*. He wondered just how bad this woman must be, to have lived so long.

'So,' she said, 'what are you doing here if you belong in Last Village?'

'We're heading north,' Ash said. It didn't seem wise to mention the Kingdom, given her reaction to the Ancestors, nor the curse that had fallen on their villages.

'Why north?'

'There's nothing to the south,' Ash said. 'We're hoping there might be something in the north.'

He listened, waiting for her response. None came. Instead, what fell from above was a thick rope. It landed with a splash.

'Not pulling you up. Sage, mage or page – you can haul yourselves out. Just be sure to tie the end around the net before you come.'

Ash reached for the rope, knotty and rough in the dimness, and searched for its end. Bronwyn had already found one of the squares at the edge of the net, and she held it out while Ash looped the rope through. He tied the knot as best he could, but it was dark and he was inexperienced in anything as practical as knot tying, and he trusted it to hold about as much as he trusted the woman up above.

'You go first,' Bronwyn said.

'Why?'

'So I can catch you if you fall. Obviously.' She patted him on the shoulder. 'If something doesn't look right up there, run. I'll be right behind you.'

Ash grasped the rope and planted his feet against the side of the pit. He walked up the wall, reaching hand over hand for the next section of rope. The earth crumbled away beneath his boots in a couple of places, but his grip was tight, and he soon regained his footing.

As he reached the top, he pulled himself closer to the wall and dragged himself on to solid ground.

The first thing he noticed was the warmth. It seemed to emanate from the ground, as though the black mulch had only just stopped smouldering. The second thing was the light: dusk had never seemed so bright. The third thing was the rope. It had not been tied around a tree stump, as he'd imagined, but was instead being held by the woman. She stood in a half-squat, a coil of the rope looped around her midriff, leaning back to maintain the tension.

The sight was enough to make Ash forget about the possibility of an ambush. He couldn't believe how strong the woman was, nor how old she looked. He'd never met anyone older than fifty-two. But this woman was like something from the Olden Days, when people had lived for centuries. She was too old to be alive.

Bronwyn emerged from the hole, and as she scrambled nimbly to her feet and glanced about, the woman began to haul up the net from the bottom of the pit. It must have weighed more than a man, drenched as it was from lying in the pool, but up it came, slithering over the edge of the pit.

Finally, she let go of the rope and tossed it on top

of the net. 'Reset that tomorrow. Too dark now.' She stepped towards Ash and Bronwyn and looked them over with cloudy eyes. 'Children you are! Come on, then. Follow me.'

She didn't wait to see if they would: she simply set off at a brisk pace. Ash and Bronwyn exchanged a glance before falling into step behind her.

The woman was small and sinewy, and wore a tattered cloak that swept the mulch behind her. She muttered continuously – to herself and the trees – and it seemed as though they moved for her; the tricking gloom made it impossible to be sure, but she never once altered her course to avoid colliding with a jagged trunk.

'Where are we going?' Bronwyn asked.

'This way,' the woman replied, unhelpfully.

They came at last to a fallen tree. It must have been a huge specimen, once upon a time, but now its severed trunk lay upended, and a wide arc of roots stood like a shield thrust into the ground. Beneath the place where the trunk met the fan of roots, a hollow had been dug in the ground. Smoke tickled Ash's throat, and he saw the remnants of a campfire smouldering in the recess, a small lidded pot hanging over the embers. Assorted rags and a patchwork quilt lay in a pile to one side.

The little woman ducked under the trunk and stoked the fire with a stick. 'Come in,' she said. 'Make yourselves at home. Another hole, I'm afraid.'

Ash and Bronwyn stooped under the trunk and squatted next to the fire. Their clothes had already begun to dry out on the walk from the pit, and now thin wisps of steam curled from their feet. The woman stacked wood on to the fire, and as the flames climbed they revealed more of her appearance. Her hair was grubby-grey and greasy, and the waxy, scarred skin of her face shone orange in the light.

'Boots off,' the woman said. 'No fun walking in wet boots.'

Ash tugged his boots off absentmindedly. Bronwyn seemed reluctant to be separated from her most valuable possessions but, after a moment's hesitation, she did the same. The woman rolled a couple of large stones from the edge of the fire and dropped them into the boots. She didn't seem to feel the heat in the palms of her hands.

'Who are you?' Bronwyn asked, her voice tinged with awe.

The woman placed the boots close to the fire and sighed. 'Haven't needed a name for a long time now.

Names are for other people to use. No people, no names. Used to be called Vivienne. Don't know if it still fits. You got that mutton?'

Ash nodded and reached for his satchel, but Vivienne waved it away with a blotchy hand.

'Keep it,' she said. 'You've a long journey, and there's plenty of food for me in these woods.'

Ash peered out into the darkness and wondered what food could possibly exist out there. He didn't have to wait long to find out. Vivienne lifted the lid off the pot and peered in at the steaming contents. Brown, slimy lumps floated in a murky broth. She replaced the lid.

'What kind of thing do you normally catch in that trap?' Bronwyn asked hesitantly, as if she was afraid of what the answer might be.

'All sorts,' Vivienne said. 'Every so often a wayward sheep falls in. That's a good day, that is! Last me for weeks and weeks, a sheep will. Used to catch plenty of dogs. Not so many nowadays. Hardly worth the butchery. Caught a fox once, too. Ever see a fox?'

Ash and Bronwyn shook their heads. The woman reached for the quilt and pointed to a patch of reddish fur.

'Beautiful creature, it was. Shame to kill it. Wouldn't have, given the choice. But it was me or the fox, so the fox got it.'

'And what's in the pot?' Bronwyn asked.

'Mushrooms. Don't need a trap to catch them.' She gave a wicked chuckle that quickly turned into a hacking cough. Finally, she spat a glob of phlegm far into the darkness. 'Lungs never been the same since the fire. Kill me eventually, it will, that fire.' She stared into the flames. 'Killed everything else.'

'Were you here when the forest burned?' Ash said. 'Is that how you . . .' His eyes flitted to her waxy skin then back to the flames.

'Don't look so bashful,' she said. 'No shame in scars. That's right. I was here.' Vivienne poked the fire with a stick. 'I burned with the trees.'

'Do you remember what happened?' Bronwyn asked. Her voice was barely audible above the crackle of the campfire.

'Course I do! Won't ever forget. Still see the inferno in my dreams, still smell the smoke when I breathe deep.' She sucked in a deep breath, as though trying to prove it. It turned into another hacking cough.

'What caused it?' Ash said. 'Helena always said—'

'Don't even mention those Ancestors! Every village is the same, always blaming gods for their misfortunes. It weren't the Ancestors: it were the sun.' She jabbed a thumb towards the black sky. 'The sun were fierce, day after day after day. No rain for weeks and weeks. Nothing unusual in that nowadays, but back then the trees were still alive and thirsty. Needed water – more water than the sky were willing to give. The leaves crunched underfoot, and the branches overhead creaked with dryness. One thing was clear to the forest folk: either it was going to rain, or it was going to burn.'

'People used to live in the forest?' Ash asked. He couldn't imagine people – a whole community – living somewhere like here: to him, it was nothing more than a wasteland.

Vivienne nodded gravely. 'The forest folk were many. Woods offered a decent living, back then. Plenty of tasty critters still hiding in the undergrowth, and the canopy shaded us from the worst of the sun. Life weren't easy, but it weren't as hard as now.'

'You were talking about how the fire started,' Bronwyn said. 'That it hadn't rained for weeks.'

'That's right. That's how it was. No rain, fierce heat. You could tell something bad were in the offing because the most secretive of critters started showing up at odd times, in broad daylight. Came to our camps, many of them did, they were that desperate to find water. But we didn't have none either. Only thing we had were clubs for breaking their poor skulls. Drank their blood – it was the only thing.'

Ash wrinkled his nose at the thought but Bronwyn stared steadily at Vivienne.

'I thought we were under attack, day the fire started. I heard a distant boom and looked up. Saw a huge cloud rolling over the treetops. Some of the folk rejoiced – thought we were saved. Clouds meant rain, you see. But then there was another boom, louder this time, and a flash of white light.'

'Lightning,' Ash whispered, remembering the bolt that had struck the weathervane in a spray of sparks.

Vivienne nodded. 'A great crackling rose up, like hundreds of feet marching through the undergrowth. Lived in fear of marauding armies back then – when people still had the energy to fight, when there were still things worth fighting for. Some thought another tribe were searching for water, forced out by the drought. But it weren't feet on the march – it were fire. When the forest is that dry, it only takes a spark.'

Vivienne lifted the lid from the pot, releasing a cloud of steam. She dipped a rough-hewn wooden spoon into the broth and took a noisy sip. 'Perfect,' she said. 'Tuck in.' She held two hollow horns beneath the surface, allowing them to fill before handing them to her guests.

Bronwyn blew steadily on the surface of her soup before taking a tentative sip. Encouraged, Ash stopped sniffing his own portion and drank a scalding mouthful. He chewed a slimy mushroom and forced it down. The soup tasted a lot like smoke, but it did a much better job of filling him up.

'Why didn't you flee?' Bronwyn asked, after a few moments of silence. 'When the fire came, why didn't you run?'

Vivienne wiped her mouth with the back of her hand. 'Can't outrun a fire, girl! Fire moves like the wind, becomes part of it. It's a fool that tries to outrun a fire, but people have always been foolish, and many tried. Didn't stand a chance. Only blessing a fire that big brings is that it's too loud to hear the screams.'

'But if you didn't run,' Ash asked, 'what did you do?'

Vivienne gazed across the fire at him. The flames writhed in her eyes, and for a heart-stopping moment Ash felt himself surrounded by the inferno.

'I did the only thing I could think to do,' Vivienne said. 'I walked into the flames.'

'But how did you survive?' Ash said.

Vivienne blew on her soup. 'Fire can't burn what's already burned. Fire goes every which way but backwards. What I did was to get behind it by going through it. Still, could've died – maybe should've. Who knows why I didn't? The forest has power – I believe that even now. Maybe it saved me because I refused to abandon it? There are saps that soothe burns, roots that store water; trees are pillars of power. But why I should survive, while so many of my betters perished, remains a mystery to me. Maybe your Ancestors can tell you that?'

Ash shuffled uncomfortably. He took a long sip of his soup. Bronwyn cleared her throat.

'Is it true – the tales they tell about what happened after the fire?'

Vivienne grinned. 'That all depends on what tales they're telling.'

'They say that it rained, and that the rains caused a great battle.'

'Then they tell the truth, but there was nothing great about it.'

'*You* witnessed the Great Battle?' Ash said. Disbelief

made his voice loud. 'My father fought at the Great Battle!'

'Then I pity your father. I hope his death was quick.'

'He didn't die. He . . .' Ash couldn't bring himself to tell Vivienne that his heroic father had gone on to abandon Last Village.

But Vivienne was lost once again in the smoke-shrouded, blood-soaked memories of her past. 'In which case, he was one of the few. The fire devoured everything in a day. All that life, living in a relay for thousands of years, dead in a single day. A black cloud hung over everything. A blanket of ash turned the world grey. And then it rained. Black rain. It was the worst thing that could have happened. The ash washed into the valleys. It poisoned the lakes. Lake Connie, Lake Wendy, Lake Esther: all turned black and scummy.

'The villages on the shores had lived in a delicate peace until that point. But suddenly they were without water. No water, no peace. They'd seen the blaze from afar, and now they went on the march, in search of someone to blame. This is where their armies converged. The smouldering forest became a battleground. It was like they were fighting for their deaths, instead of fighting for their lives. It was like they knew there was no future worth living for.'

Ash and Bronwyn sat in silence. Even the campfire had settled into a noiseless, pulsating glow.

'I was propped against a tree. Watched it all unfold. I think those who saw me mistook me for a corpse. For a while, I wished they were right.'

The fire collapsed in on itself with a soft, crumbling sound. It seemed to stir Vivienne from her reverie.

'Enough of the past,' she said, throwing a handful of bark on the fire. It let out a pungent aroma that dispelled the gathering mosquitoes. 'If the Ancestors didn't get their fill of revenge that day, I don't know when they ever will.'

Ash looked down at his bare feet. For as long as he could remember, the Ancestors had been the governing force in his life: they rewarded every sacrifice in their honour and punished every misdeed. They were fickle and cruel and omnipotent, and yet Vivienne seemed able to criticise them with impunity.

Perhaps surviving is her punishment, Ash thought, looking around the hole in which she lived. *Perhaps the Ancestors will keep her alive until she repents.*

And yet, he could not imagine Vivienne ever repenting.

'Time to sleep,' she said. 'You must be tired.'

Ash and Bronwyn did not argue. They curled up on

the ground, facing the fire. Both clutched their satchels to their bodies, although it was hard to imagine who might take them in the night.

Vivienne remained sitting, clutching her knees and staring into the fire.

'Aren't you going to sleep?' Ash said, his eyelids drooping.

Vivienne shook her head. 'Not yet. I'm going to speak to the ghosts. Stories stir them, and stories still them. It's cruel to wake the dead and not lay them to rest again.'

Ash nodded, sleepily. He was too tired to decide whether he believed in ghosts or not. And so he fell asleep to the sound of Vivienne's voice, mumbling in the darkness, to an audience of one, or one thousand.

9

Vivienne was still talking when Ash and Bronwyn woke in the morning. She appeared to be talking to herself. They sat up just as she removed the pot from the fire.

'Soup's ready,' she said.

Ash wasn't sure whether he could stomach slimy mushrooms first thing in the morning, but he knew he had to eat: Vivienne's hospitality might be the last they encountered for some time. He took the drinking horn and raised it to his lips. When he swallowed the soup, he swallowed a rising queasiness with it.

'Boots are dry,' Vivienne said. 'Going to be another hot day, too.'

Ash and Bronwyn followed her gaze. The sun sat low in a cloudless sky: shafts of golden light sliced between the trees. It made Ash think of Helena's prophecy.

Is it really possible for the sun to disappear?

Vivienne caught him looking at the sun and seemed

to read his mind. 'Did Helena ever finish her almanac?' she asked.

Ash was taken aback. He hadn't expected anyone else to know about her project. The surprise must have been visible on his face, because Vivienne grinned a toothless grin.

'She were a smart girl. I remember her mentor giving her the task of interpreting the sun. He said only the brightest pupil could understand something so bright. Clever man. Spoke clever.' She sighed. 'Dead now. Death was cleverer.'

'Was Helena raised here?' Ash said. He'd assumed that Vivienne knew Helena from her occasional wanderings, but now he began to suspect their relationship went deeper than that.

'Indeed. A woodswoman through and through. Sent away to another village – your village – to be their priestess, years before the fire. Saved her life, that did.' She looked at the sun again. 'A fool's errand, if you ask me. The sun is the sun. Nothing more to know.'

'She predicted that it would disappear,' Ash said. 'Tomorrow.'

Vivienne looked at Ash with her milky eyes. 'Is that so? And you expect some sort of reckoning, I suppose?'

Bronwyn said nothing. Ash cleared his throat.

'That will be the sign that our suffering is over. It's why we're heading to the Kingdom.' He paused, braced for a scornful reply, but Vivienne said nothing. 'Have you heard of it?'

Vivienne narrowed her eyes. Then she tossed a couple of branches on the fire and stood up. 'Finish your soup,' she said, 'and follow me.'

She did not wait, just strode away from the shelter of the toppled tree. Ash and Bronwyn downed the last of their soup, pulled on their boots, picked up their satchels and set off after her. They hadn't gone far when they came to a slab of rock that jutted up from the mulch. Vivienne stood beside it, placing pebbles on the pitted stone.

'We're here,' she said, pointing to the base of the slab. 'At the northern tip of the forest you'll come to the Drowned Village – or Lowdale, to give its proper name. Nobody lived there last time I checked, but that were years ago.' Vivienne's finger moved further up the slab and hovered over a grey pebble. 'Next, you'll come to the caves overlooking Lowdale. Used to be a good place to rest, those caves, from the sun or a storm. Not visited for many years so couldn't vouch for them now.' Her crooked fingers indicated another stone. 'Beyond the caves is the Pikes.'

'The Pikes?' Ash said, confused.

'Yes, the Pikes. Mountains. Big rocky things with pointy tips.'

'I know what a mountain is,' Ash said. What he did not say was that mountains had only ever been a dark tear at the hem of the sky's skirts. They were low, small things to his mind. 'We just have a different name for them.'

'Oh, aye? And what do you call them?'

'The Nameless Mountains.'

Vivienne snorted. 'Sounds to me like someone didn't know what to call them.'

'You were telling us about the journey north,' Bronwyn said.

'Aye, I was. Mines is the shortest route through the Pikes, but you mustn't use that path. Stay out of the mines. If you go in, you won't come out.'

'Why not?' Ash said. 'What's in the mines?'

'Plenty of rumours about the mines, but can't trust a rumour. Still, none of them are good, so maybe there's something in that.'

'What kind of rumours?' Ash said. It seemed important

to at least know what people were making up about the place. Not that he had any intention of finding out how true the rumours were.

Vivienne huffed. Clearly, she deemed gossip and rumours beneath her. 'Monsters, half-creatures, bottomless pits, endless passageways. That's what folks say, but it's probably just fear talking. No one's gone through there in years. Don't matter either way – you need to go over the mountains, not through them.' She stared meaningfully at Ash and Bronwyn. 'Stay out of the mines.'

They nodded and quickly directed their attention to the next marker: a stone so pale it might have been bone.

'Is that the Kingdom?' Ash said hopefully.

'That's the rumour.'

'I thought you couldn't trust a rumour?'

'You can't.'

'So you don't know?'

'You're talking about a place that exists in stories. A dream place. *Nobody* knows. Most of what I've told you so far is based on hearsay and whispers, spoken by people long since dead. Have you thought about what you'll do if all you find is abandoned villages and dry riverbeds?'

'No.' Ash shook his head. 'That won't happen. I know it won't.'

Vivienne raised her bald eyebrows. 'And why not?'

Ash glanced at Bronwyn. 'It has been foretold. The Ancestors will call us to the Kingdom when our suffering is over.'

'Well, then,' Vivienne said, gathering up the stones and dropping them into deep pockets. 'Let us hope that your suffering is almost at an end. North is that way.' She gave a quick nod, then turned to leave.

'Wait,' Bronwyn said.

She turned back.

'Can you tell us anything else?'

Vivienne looked to the trees, as though they were her advisors.

'Yes. No one is to be trusted – especially anyone with enough to share.'

'What about you?' Ash said. 'We trusted you.'

'No.' Vivienne grinned. 'I trusted you.'

Rays of hot sunlight broke from behind a thick trunk, prompting Vivienne to glance over her shoulder into the glare. 'Time to get gone,' she said, withdrawing a small sack from inside her cloak. 'Here. Hope you like mushrooms.'

Bronwyn caught the bag and stuffed it hastily inside her satchel. 'Thank you.'

Vivienne waved a hand. 'No bother. Good luck to you both.'

She began to walk away, back to her hovel.

'Wait,' Bronwyn said again. Vivienne stopped and turned.

'Why don't you come with us?'

'Couldn't do that,' she said, with a smile. 'Got to be someone here to keep the ghosts company. Got to be someone here to watch for the first leaf.' She made to go, but hesitated. 'Never asked your names. Lost me manners in the fire. What names should I listen for when they write songs about your escapades?'

'Bronwyn.'

'And you?'

'Ash.'

Vivienne's smile faltered for a moment, but then it returned, slyer than ever. 'Your father fought here, you say?'

Ash nodded.

'And I suspect you were born soon afterwards?'

'Yes. Why?'

'You were named after this place, young Ash.' She

110

leaned closer and lowered her voice. 'You were forged in fire.' She flashed a wicked smile then turned away, her cloak dragging a swathe through the blackened debris.

'Stop!' Ash called. 'What does that mean?'

But Vivienne kept walking, and soon the trees conspired to hide her.

'We'd better move,' Bronwyn said, setting off. 'The day will only get hotter.'

Ash adjusted the straps across his chest and scurried after her. 'What do you think she meant?' he asked. *Forged in fire.*

'I don't know.' Bronwyn quickened her pace, weaving a path between the blackened trunks. 'Let's just focus on moving north.'

Ash fell silent, turning the words over like a knot that had been tied too tight. After several minutes of walking in silence, the sweat was pouring from them both.

'Wouldn't it make sense to walk at night?' he asked, wiping his face with a sleeve. 'Cooler, I mean, and less chance of meeting people?'

'No,' Bronwyn said. 'Nights are for hiding from things that can see in the dark.'

Ash swallowed, and nearly choked on the dryness. 'What things?'

'Let's just say that Vivienne isn't the only one who's heard rumours about half-creatures.'

Ash glanced around the decimated forest. Their slushy footsteps were the only sound. He found it impossible to decide which would be worse: a world devoid of people, or a world in which some of the people might be monsters.

It took another three hours of brisk walking to reach the northern edge of the Burned Forest. They came to a stop, looking out over hills that rose around a dusty plain. On the horizon, the jagged peaks of the Pikes loomed up, black even where the sunlight touched them.

'Here,' Bronwyn said, holding out a hand for the waterskin. Ash lifted the strap over his head and passed it to Bronwyn. 'One mouthful,' she said, removing the stopper. 'Hold it in your mouth and breathe through your nose. It helps with the thirst.'

Bronwyn lifted the sack of water to her lips, careful not to spill a drop. She passed it back to Ash, who did the same. Afterwards, they both stood there with bloated cheeks, looking down into the sun-scorched valley.

In the distance, a dense clump of houses huddled on the valley floor: Lowdale. It looked as deserted as

Vivienne had suggested, but there was only one way to be sure. Bronwyn adjusted the strap of her satchel, took a deep breath, and began the descent.

The slope was dry and crumbly, and soon a veneer of dust clung to the sweat on their arms. The sun beat down. The water in Ash's cheeks turned warm as spit, and resisting the temptation to swallow required all of his willpower.

They rejoined the river at the foot of the hill, stepping over stones that had been washed smooth by centuries of water – now dusty and hot and baked by the sun. The valley was deathly quiet, and yet it was impossible to believe they were alone. Ash felt watched, and it was a feeling that grew heavier than anything else he carried.

Eventually, the narrow entrance to the valley widened to reveal the shabby village of Lowdale. The houses were squat and dilapidated and packed together. The lanes between them were narrow and labyrinthine. All was still.

Heat rose from the cracked ground in shimmering waves, stirring the tips of Ash's hair. He stared at something that lay against the buckled roof of a church, near the centre of the village. He swallowed his mouthful of water, warm and thick.

'What is that?' Ash said.

Bronwyn swallowed. 'I think it's a boat.'

'A what?'

'A boat. Something people used to travel across water.'

Ash looked at the long wooden object; it did not look like something that could float. 'What's it doing here? And how did it get up there?' He looked to the sky, as though it might have fallen in the last downpour.

'They dammed the river, back in the Olden Days, to create a new lake. The village of Lowdale was here before the waters rose, and it's here now they've gone.'

'People could do that, back then?'

'That and more.'

Ash tried to imagine twenty fathoms of water above him but it was, like so much else about the past, impossible.

They walked amongst the houses, listening for something beyond the scuff of their own footsteps. They did not expect to hear anything – the place was deserted – so the voice came as a shock.

'Children, Mart! Come and see the children!'

Ash and Bronwyn turned to see an elderly woman standing in a doorway. She held her hands clasped beneath her chin. The skin of her arms was soft with wrinkles and bronzed by the sun. Tears sparkled in her eyes. 'Come quickly, Mart!'

'I'm coming,' said a faltering voice from inside. 'Just give me a moment, Gwen.'

A man appeared beside the woman. He squinted as though the children had been spotted on a distant hillside. His bushy grey eyebrows met above his nose.

'Are they real, Mart? Tell me they're real.'

'Are you real?' Mart asked in a stern voice.

Ash and Bronwyn exchanged a glance. 'Yes,' Bronwyn said. 'We're real.'

Mart turned to Gwen. 'She says they're real.'

Gwen clapped her hands together and let out a little shriek. 'I don't know how long it's been since I last saw children. How long has it been, Mart?'

'I don't know. A long time.'

'Such a long, long time.' Gwen bit her lip with a toothless gum. 'Where are your parents, children?'

Ash and Bronwyn shared another glance. 'We don't have any,' Bronwyn said.

Ash looked at Bronwyn with newfound sympathy; he had not known she was an orphan too.

'Poor mites,' Gwen said. She wrung her hands. 'Did you hear that, Mart? They're all alone.'

Mart grunted. 'Terrible.'

'They need looking after. Come inside, children, out of the sun. You look like you've been trekking for days.'

'No, thank you,' said Bronwyn. 'We've got to get going.'

'You're both so skinny,' Gwen said. 'We have plenty to eat. Mart and I don't need much. We're happy to share, aren't we, Mart?'

Mart grunted again. He seemed to be studying the sky.

'Really,' Ash said. 'It's fine.'

'We used to have grandchildren.' Gwen shook her head. 'They were taken from us.'

'Taken?' Bronwyn asked. 'By who?'

'Men from the north. They took most of the village and killed anyone who resisted. Left the useless ones behind.'

Mart wiped his eye with a trembling knuckle.

'Come inside,' Gwen said, beckoning them forward. 'You don't have to stay for long – just long enough to remind us of what we used to have.'

Ash looked at Gwen's pleading eyes. No one had ever wanted him so badly, and the thought of being taken in and fed and cared for – after everything he'd lost and endured – was too much to resist. He glanced at Bronwyn, and although her face remained blank, her stomach gurgled audibly at the promise of food.

He looked back at Gwen. She gave a small smile that was full of pain. Ash took a step forwards.

'Come,' Gwen said. Her eyes darted to the slack waterskin Ash wore across his chest. 'We have water. Lots of water.' Ash took another step forward. Gwen licked her lips and smiled. 'You can drink as much as you like.'

The muscles at the corner of Gwen's mouth twitched. Ash stopped. Gwen frowned, but her smile remained. Her cheeks started to spasm. Ash knew then that he did not want to enter the house. He suspected that if they went in they would never come out. He knew what it was like to pretend to be happy. He had fixed a smile on his face for most of his childhood.

He remembered Vivienne's warning: *No one is to be trusted – especially anyone with enough to share.*

'No,' he said, taking a step backwards. 'No, thank you.'

The smile began to slip from Gwen's face. 'Come. You shouldn't be out here on your own. It's dangerous.'

'We'll take our chances,' Ash said.

He turned and walked around the side of the house with Bronwyn close behind.

'What made you change your mind?' Bronwyn asked in a low voice.

Ash shrugged. 'I don't know. It just didn't seem right.'

'We do need more water.'

'I know. But do you really think they have enough to share?'

Bronwyn opened her mouth, but it was another voice that spoke. They turned around. Gwen and Mart stood at the back door of the house.

'Children,' Gwen said, her voice breaking as she strained to shout. 'Won't you come back? Please?'

'No,' Ash said. 'There's somewhere else we need to be. I'm sorry.'

The hope in Gwen's glistening eyes faded, and it was replaced by a look so spiteful it took Ash's breath away. Or perhaps what made him gasp was the pile of bones in the backyard. Large bones. Too large to have come from a sheep.

Or perhaps it was the rope coiled around Mart's hand. The sight of him stooping to untether something that pulled the rope taut, something the colour of rust – something that longed to be . . . unleashed.

A dog bolted from the house. Thick strings of drool flew from its yellow fangs. Heavy paws thudded against the ground. Vicious claws churned chunks of dry earth up into the air.

'Go on!' Mart shouted. 'Get!'

Ash and Bronwyn ran. They fled between the derelict buildings, hurtling along alleyways and around blind corners. Ragged, panicky breaths bounced between the walls. Behind them, the dog snarled and growled and barked.

'This way,' Bronwyn said, reaching out a hand and dragging Ash towards the church. They ran beneath the hull of the stranded boat, darted along a narrow alley, and suddenly found themselves out in the open. There were no more houses. Before them was half a mile of cracked earth and a range of hills. High above, two black holes were set into the hillside like empty eye sockets.

'The caves!' Ash shouted. 'We need to reach the caves!'

Bronwyn was fast. She had already edged ahead of Ash. Paws thundered behind him, growing louder with every second. He glanced back and wished that he hadn't. The dog was closing in. Ash looked ahead and knew that he would be caught before he reached the hills.

He fumbled at his waist for Kelly's club. It snagged on his cord belt. He yanked and the force of it coming free threw him off balance. He staggered, caught himself, and turned to face the dog.

Paws the size of fists slammed into his chest, knocking him backwards. The club flew from his hand and skittered along the ground. He tried to call out – to scream – but the dog had crushed the air from his lungs. A pair of snapping, slobbery jaws lunged at his face, and Ash only just managed to get his hands around the dog's throat in time. The stink of rotten meat and unwashed fur filled his nostrils. Hot drool landed on his cheek and pooled in his ear. The dog lunged again, raking its claws across Ash's chest. Its red-rimmed eyes glared like those of a demon.

Ash fought to keep the vicious teeth at arm's length, but the dog was strong and his grip was loosening. The next bite snapped just inches above his throat. Ash tried to wriggle free but it only drove the claws deeper into his flesh. The pain made him weak, and the scent of blood made the dog strong. Ash could feel the power ebbing from his arms. His right hand slipped. A small sound of defeat and terror – a dying sound – escaped from his throat.

Ash closed his eyes.

The dog bared its teeth and lunged.

A high yelp filled the air and echoed around the vast bowl of the valley. Ash opened his eyes. Bronwyn stood over him, clutching the club. Ash dragged himself on to his elbows and watched the dog turn in a clumsy circle, its head and tail hanging low. It staggered and whined and came very close to falling in the dust. It shook its mangy coat and cast a sly glance at its prey. Then it trotted back towards the shabby dwellings of Lowdale.

'Can you stand?' Bronwyn asked.

Ash had no desire to stand. He wanted to lie down for a long time and rest until his heart descended from his throat to his chest. But he knew that couldn't happen. There might be more people, or more dogs, and the heat – completely forgotten during the attack – would soon succeed where the dog had failed.

'Help me up,' he said.

Bronwyn reached down and hauled him to his feet.

'Thanks,' he said. It had never seemed such a puny, inadequate word.

Bronwyn shrugged. 'Don't mention it. I only came back because you've got the water.'

Ash tried to laugh, but his tender ribcage cut it short. He lifted his shirt to wipe the sweat and dust and drool from his face and found it spotted with blood.

'Are you okay?' Bronwyn asked.

'I'm fine.'

He looked back at Lowdale, shimmering like a mirage. The dog, no more than a wet speck, disappeared between the buildings.

'I think we made the right decision back there,' Ash said.

'You think?' She handed him the club. 'Here.'

'Let's hope I get to use it next time,' Ash said.

Bronwyn raised an eyebrow. 'Let's hope there isn't a next time.'

10

The caves did not look inviting. It was impossible to tell from a distance whether they were the refuge that Vivienne had known, and even at the threshold they refused to give up their secrets.

Ash and Bronwyn stood at the entrance to the right-hand cave and peered into the gloom, scattering a mischief of rats into the darkest corners. Somewhere, water *drip-drip-drip*ped with a fragile echo. A hot wind whistled over the rocks high above, but not so much as a ripple disturbed the pool that stretched deep into the cave.

'Water,' Ash said.

Bronwyn nodded, her expression grim. 'Water means people.'

'Should we go in?'

Bronwyn shrugged. 'We don't have much choice. We need to rest.'

They took a step inside.

'Can you see how far back it goes?' Ash whispered. In the echoey stillness, his voice sounded loud and brash.

'Not quite. Hang on.' Bronwyn reached down and collected a flat stone from the ground. She threw it deep into the darkness and listened. After a second or so, they heard it hit the water with a gulp. 'Hmm,' Bronwyn said. 'It goes further than I thought. I was hoping the stone would hit the back wall.'

'Why don't we just shelter by the entrance?' Ash said. The quietness was beginning to unnerve him.

'I'm not spending the night in a cave if I don't know what else is hiding in it.'

Ash opened his mouth to protest, but it was hard to argue with such a sensible rule.

Bronwyn strode further into the cave. When she reached the edge of the pool, she dropped her satchel to the ground and hopped on to the first of a series of stepping stones that led into the darkness. As she moved from one stone to the next, she stopped and peered into the depths of the cave. After just three steps it was difficult for Ash to pick her out in the gloom.

'Bronwyn,' he said. He took a step towards the pool to keep her in sight – to reassure himself as much as for any other reason. 'Bronwyn, don't go too far.'

'I think I can see the back. There's a darker patch where the water ends. There's light too – over there. I think the two caves must be connected.'

'Bronwyn.' Ash's voice was amplified by the cave, and so was the fear in it. 'Bronwyn, come back.'

He took another step forward and something crunched beneath his boot.

'I told you,' Bronwyn said. 'I'm not staying here until I know we're alone.' She stepped on to the next stone. 'Hey, there are *fish* in this pool.'

'Bronwyn. Come back.'

Bronwyn caught the tremor in Ash's voice. She turned on the spot to look back at him. He seemed further away than was possible, but she could see that his attention was fixed on his feet.

'What is it?' she asked. Her lonely voice was dwarfed by its own echo.

Ash tilted his foot to the side, and there beneath his sole was a pile of tiny bones. Scraps of flesh still clung to them. The stones beneath were slick with blood. The meal was fresh. It had been abandoned – interrupted, perhaps – and so recently that the rats hadn't picked the bones clean yet.

Interrupted by us, Ash thought.

Bronwyn came back to the shore and looked at the mess of fragile bones.

'Perhaps we shouldn't stay here,' Ash said. 'We don't know who else is using this cave.'

'We need to rest. Besides, it's empty now. We'll just have to hope whoever was here doesn't come back.' She returned to the pool and scooped a handful of water to her mouth. 'Tastes good. We should fill the skin now, in case we need to leave in a hurry.'

Ash obeyed, removing the stopper and holding the spout beneath the water. As he did so, a school of pale fish darted away. He watched them intently. He had never seen a live fish before.

'Do you know how to catch one?' Bronwyn asked.

Ash shook his head. 'No.' He watched the fish swim in a lazy circle. 'And I'm not sure whether I'd want to, even if I could.'

The fish moved like water, and they shone like fragments of light. Ash kept the skin below the water long after it had filled, so as not to scare them away.

'I think we should stay,' Bronwyn said.

Ash sighed and stoppered the waterskin. The fish disappeared in a flash. He reached down a hand and scooped cool water into his mouth. It soothed his scratchy throat. 'Are you sure?'

'Where else is there to go? We'll soon reach the Pikes and who knows how long it will take to cross them. Do we really want to get there just as night is falling?'

They both looked out at the coming dusk. The low sun threw long shadows across the valley, and the purplish sky washed the distant buildings of Lowdale in a supernatural light.

'At least here we've got a view of the valley. We'll be able to see anyone coming from the south for miles.'

'What if they come from the north?' Ash said.

They both looked at the pile of bones, and the rats picking them clean.

'There's water here,' Bronwyn said, not even trying to answer Ash's question.

'Which makes it even more likely that people will come here. You said so yourself.'

'We'll just have to take our chances, but we should take it in turns to sleep, just in case.'

Ash took a deep breath. 'Fine.'

They gathered up their things and moved to the mouth of the cave. It was lighter there, and less dank, and felt less like being entombed than dwelling in the depths. They found two flat slabs of rock and lay down to rest.

'You go first,' Bronwyn said.

Ash knew he should protest, but he simply didn't have the strength. 'Okay,' he said. 'But make sure you wake me up.'

'I will.'

Ash put the plump waterskin under his head and closed his eyes. The rock slab might as well have been a thick woollen fleece for all he noticed it. The scratches on his chest tingled in a far-off way that made him think of mosquito bites. He couldn't think of mosquito bites without thinking of his mother, and for once he didn't feel the need to chase such thoughts away. She would be waiting for him in the Kingdom – his father too. He smiled.

'What is it?' Bronwyn asked.

The sound of her voice startled Ash, but not enough to rouse him.

'I was just thinking about the Kingdom.' His smile widened. 'All the water you can drink, feasts every day, no chores to be done. All the people you ever loved waiting to embrace you.'

There was a long silence, broken by the steady *drip-*

drip-drip from the roof. Ash felt himself sinking into the rock. He had almost forgotten about Bronwyn by the time she spoke again. Her voice was soft and uncertain.

'What if the Kingdom doesn't exist?' she asked.

'Blasphemy,' Ash said, sleepily. 'Of course the Kingdom exists.'

'But what if it doesn't?'

Ash frowned. It felt like someone was dragging him out of a deep and cosy den, and he was not ready to face the light. 'Has to,' he said. 'Was foretold. The Ancestors . . .' Ash trailed off. Sleep was pulling him under.

'What if it's just a story, and there's nothing in the north but more of the same?' Bronwyn said. 'You heard what that woman, Gwen, said about the abductions in Lowdale; what if that's what happened in our villages?'

'No,' Ash said. He wasn't sure whether he was dreaming or not. 'She was lying. You saw the bones.'

Bronwyn fell silent. She had seen the bones.

A minute later, Ash was asleep.

11

Tired as they were, Ash and Bronwyn did not linger in the cave. When Ash woke up from his third nap, just before dawn, he found Bronwyn attempting to catch a fish. She lay very still at the pool's edge, cupping her hands beneath the surface, but it quickly became apparent that fish were not as gullible as she had hoped and she soon gave it up. When there was enough light to see by they filled their stomachs with water from the pool, slung their satchels across their bodies, and stepped out into the dawn.

The air hung hot and still; within minutes, their backs were tickly with sweat. They descended the northern slope of the hill and trekked along a rocky, boulder-strewn path that had once been a river. The steep slopes on either side were treacherous with scree. Up ahead, the Pikes loomed like the jagged teeth of a vicious trap. They walked one behind the other, their eyes continuously scanning the rocky slopes: partly for a higher path, partly for people.

'Helena used to say there were tarns in the highest hills,' Ash said. 'Some as big as lakes.'

'We have water,' Bronwyn said.

'I know. That's not what I meant.'

Bronwyn glanced back. 'You're thinking about what might live here?'

Ash nodded.

'Well, don't. They're rumours, that's all. There's no need for us to make them any more than that.'

But for all her brave talk and scorn of superstition, Bronwyn kept her eyes trained on the slopes and spoke in low whispers.

The dry riverbed began to widen, and they advanced towards the mountains side by side. They came to rest beneath a spindly tree that had somehow managed to survive the storms that had toppled its neighbours. They drank, but it did little to quench their thirst. They ate, but it only seemed to intensify their hunger. The sun rested high in the sky. The heat was unrelenting.

'I don't know if we'll be able to cross the Pikes before nightfall,' Bronwyn said, 'but I think we should keep walking until we reach the other side – even if it means walking through the night. The less time we spend among the Pikes, the better.'

Ash nodded. 'Agreed. How long—' A distant scream interrupted him. 'What was that?'

'Shh,' said Bronwyn, straining to hear. Low voices were chanting something incomprehensible. They seemed to be coming from higher up the mountainside. There was another scream.

'Gather up our things,' Ash said. 'Quickly. We'll try to find a passage further east.'

Bronwyn froze with her satchel strap above her head. 'Shouldn't we find out what's happening?' she asked.

'It doesn't sound like anything good.'

Ash rose and made to move away, but Bronwyn grabbed his arm.

'Someone is in trouble,' she said.

'And we'll be in trouble too, if we don't keep clear.'

There was another scream, and it unnerved Ash. He shook his head, as though trying to dislodge an unwanted thought.

'If it was one of us,' Bronwyn said, 'we'd want someone to help.'

Ash thought of all the times he'd needed help and been left to face his problems alone. It didn't seem fair to risk his chance of reaching the Kingdom by trying to save someone else. And yet, abandoning them didn't seem fair, either.

He sighed. He looked up at the towering mountains and then closed his eyes. 'Fine,' he said. 'We'll take a look. But we might not be able to help.'

The chanting came again, the low voices growing louder as Ash and Bronwyn crept up the foot of the mountain to investigate. The ground was strewn with brittle branches that threatened to betray their approach, and each broken tree trunk suddenly seemed to resemble a person. They kept low, constantly surveying the ground and the slope ahead.

And all the while the voices got louder, until they felt sure they must somehow be amongst them.

The mountainside suddenly levelled off. Ash and Bronwyn found themselves at the edge of a small plateau and ducked behind a desiccated bush. Before them was a wide circle of upright stones – most of them taller than men – that had somehow been dragged up the mountainside, or brought down from above, and placed evenly apart. In front of each stone, a figure stood beside a flaming torch, dressed in a hooded cloak of brown wool. And at the centre of the circle, tethered to the largest rock of all, was a boy in the shabbiest clothing Ash or Bronwyn had ever seen: everything except for his brilliant blond hair was dark with grime and dirt. He couldn't have been older than seven years old.

'Who is he, do you think?' Bronwyn whispered.

Ash shook his head. 'I don't know, and we're not going to find out. Come on.'

'Wait,' Bronwyn hissed. 'Maybe we can help.'

'No.'

'Why not?'

'Can you count?'

'Of course I can count.'

'Good. Start counting the people wearing cloaks.'

Bronwyn looked back at the circle of druidic figures. One of them stood apart, near the central stone, swinging a smoking lantern on the end of a chain. The chanting matched its steady rhythm: up and down, up and down.

'How many?' Ash asked.

'I don't understand,' Bronwyn said. 'What's the use in counting them? We need to do something.'

'How many?' Ash asked again.

Bronwyn muttered something under her breath, but she began to count. 'Thirteen.'

'Correct.'

Bronwyn shot Ash a sidelong scowl.

'Now, how many of me can you see?'

'What?'

'I don't know why you're confused – this one's easier.'

'One,' she said. 'There's one of you.'

'Right again.'

'What's your point?'

'If it takes you longer to count your enemies than your allies, it's probably best not to pick a fight.'

Bronwyn continued to scowl.

'Come on,' Ash said. 'We've wasted too much time already. They won't be distracted by this ritual for ever, and if they find us we'll be next.'

He tried to move away from the cover of the bush, but once again Bronwyn caught him by the arm.

'What now?' Ash said.

It was Bronwyn's turn to ask infuriating questions. 'Do you know what they're doing?'

'Nothing worth sticking around to watch.'

'They're going to sacrifice him, aren't they?'

Ash glared at Bronwyn, and was surprised to see that her face was blank and calm. He pursed his lips and stared at a tree that was not worth staring at.

'Yes,' he said. It was like chewing on a bitter root. 'I think so.'

Bronwyn swallowed. 'Who to?'

Ash hesitated, even though the answer was waiting on his tongue, ready to be spoken.

The Ancestors.

The realisation was like being crushed by one of the standing stones. To help the boy would mean defying the Ancestors, and to defy the Ancestors would be to earn their wrath and displeasure. He glanced around: over his shoulder, he had an expansive view of the dusty, barren hills. It was punishment made permanent. It was vengeance carved into earth and stone. Nothing lived: only the forgotten survived. The whole landscape was testament to the Ancestors' power. Only a fool would stand against them.

And yet it did not seem right to abandon the boy; Ash knew all too well how it felt to be abandoned.

I'd be just like my father, he thought, *deserting the person who needs me most.*

The chanting had stopped. The mountain was deathly quiet. No one moved on the plateau: it was as if the druids had turned to stone themselves. The only thing that could be heard was the little boy's panicked breathing.

'They're waiting,' Ash said. 'They're waiting for something.'

'Well, we're not. We've got to go. We waited too long.'

Bronwyn made to move, but a growing darkness made her freeze. It was as though the afternoon was ageing impossibly fast, as though a giant had thrown his cloak over the world, as though some unimaginable power was summoning night.

'What's happening?' Bronwyn asked.

A smile spread across Ash's face: Helena had been right. 'The sun.'

He watched as the circle of druids lowered their heads, and the leader's swinging lantern came to a stop. An unnatural darkness fell. It was almost total. The boy bound to the rock began to insult his captors as loudly and creatively as he could. He knew a surprising amount of swear words for a seven-year-old.

'This is our chance,' Ash said. 'Come on.'

Bronwyn grabbed Ash by the sleeve and dragged him back into the cover of the bush.

'What are you doing?' she said.

'Don't you see? The Ancestors are helping us. They want us to save him.'

'But we'll be seen!'

'The Ancestors won't let that happen. Come on. We don't have much time.'

Bronwyn opened her mouth but all that came out was a sigh. Ash stood up, pulled his arm free from Bronwyn's grasp, and strode towards the stone circle. The darkness concealed his approach, but only partially, and a thrill of panic shot through him as he passed between two stones. He glanced up at the sun – a black disc surrounded by a golden halo – and quickened his pace.

The boy tied to the rock didn't spot Ash until he was a couple of paces away. He mistook him for a druid, or the recipient of his sacrifice, and began to curse with renewed enthusiasm.

'Hold still,' Ash said, picking at the knots that held him.

Puzzled, the boy stopped shouting, and the sudden silence fell on Ash like a darker shadow.

'Keep shouting,' he whispered. 'Otherwise they'll get suspicious.'

The boy let out a fresh volley of abuse, and it wasn't until Bronwyn appeared beside Ash that he understood why it sounded so genuine: she was carrying a small knife clutched in her hand.

'Where did you get that?' Ash said.

'There's no time to explain,' she said, 'and there's no time for knots either.' She began sawing through the rope.

The boy had stopped shouting again. Ash glanced around at the druids. They could have been statues they stood so still, but he knew it wouldn't last. A thin crescent of the sun was already beginning to reappear.

One of the ropes fell to the ground, and Bronwyn began to hack at another.

'Hurry,' Ash said, grappling with a knot at the boy's ankles.

'Who are you?' the boy asked. His voice was almost as threadbare as his clothes.

'We'll explain later,' Ash said. 'Is that loose enough? Can you free your foot?'

The boy tried to lift his leg, and after a few sharp pulls he worked his right foot free. A few seconds later, and he stood apart from the rock with only one arm tethered to it.

Bronwyn hacked at the taut rope. Light was returning to the landscape. It would be a matter of seconds before the druids lifted their heads and witnessed their sacrifice being cut free.

'There,' Bronwyn said, casting the severed rope aside.

The three of them turned to run back down the mountainside and stopped. The druids had lowered their hoods. They stood watching the three children with cold eyes. Their heads were shaven, their faces expressionless. They reminded Ash of the maimed statue in the village graveyard.

And then, they began to approach.

Ash and Bronwyn edged backwards, towards the towering wall of rock. Bronwyn held out her knife and Ash brandished his club, but the circle of druids kept advancing. The little boy snatched a flaming torch from beside the central rock and swung it from side to side.

'We're trapped,' Bronwyn said.

Ash glanced behind and saw a dark hole in the mountainside. A pair of tracks led inside beneath a thick wooden lintel. A thorn of fear pressed against his heart. The rectangle of darkness was impenetrable. It occupied space like a physical thing. And it was towards this oblivion that they were being shepherded.

Ash realised, too late, that the druids had intended to send their captive into the mines all along: the very place to which he was now being ushered.

Bronwyn caught sight of the entrance, and Ash's gaze fixed upon it.

'No,' she said.

Ash looked to the druids, the gaps between them shrinking with every step they took. 'It's our only option.'

They continued to edge backwards, the boy swinging his torch in a wide, flaming arc. The druids were now shoulder to shoulder in a tight semicircle. Ash sensed the opening behind him, felt the darkness pulling him in.

The druids began to chant, but all Ash could hear were Vivienne's words, repeated over and over in her croaky, smoky voice.

Stay out of the mines.

Stay out of the mines.

Stay out of the mines.

But there was only one way out.

They took a step back.

And the mountain swallowed them.

12

The air was so chill it made the three children gasp. Ash had never known cold like it. A fresh breeze swept past them, turning Ash's sweat to ice water beneath his clothes. Their breath clouded before their faces in the torchlight.

'Ho!' Bronwyn said, wrapping her arms around her chest and tucking her hands under her armpits. 'Ho!'

'Uh,' Ash said. All his life he'd longed for something other than unrelenting heat. Seconds before, he would have welcomed the cold, but now he could only grunt in shock.

'Do either of you know the mines?' the boy asked, fidgeting from foot to foot.

Ash and Bronwyn shook their heads. They were both too busy trying to stop their teeth from chattering to speak.

'Me neither,' the boy said. 'Still, not like we can go

back out there. Thanks, by the way, for helping me.'

'You're welcome,' Ash mumbled. He was regretting it already.

Bronwyn managed to control her shivering just enough to ask: 'Who are you?'

'Samuel,' the boy said with a sudden, gummy grin. 'What are your names?'

They told him, and the boy repeated the names aloud, as if to practise.

'Do you think we'll be friends?' Samuel asked.

'If we make it out of this mine,' Ash said, 'we'll basically be family.'

Samuel's grin widened. 'I've never had a family. You can be my mummy and daddy.'

Ash and Bronwyn exchanged a glance.

'I was thinking more like siblings,' Ash said.

'Okay! I've always wanted a brother and a sister. Here.' Samuel held out the torch to Ash. 'You should be the leader. That's what big brothers are for.'

Ash reluctantly accepted the torch and lifted it as high as the low ceiling would allow. A long tunnel burrowed into the mountainside, stretching further than the flickering light could reach. The walls on either side were not solid slabs of rock, but instead comprised innumerable pieces of slate that had been neatly stacked by ancient hands. Long ago, carts loaded with stone had been pushed from the dark depths out into the light. The grooves they had worn into the ground offered some reassurance that the tunnel led *somewhere*, but not much and, soon enough, the tracks disappeared altogether beneath spills of broken stone.

'The sooner we set off,' Ash said, 'the sooner we find a way out.'

Bronwyn and Samuel said nothing. Ash filled his lungs with the icy air, adjusted his grip on the torch, and took his first step into the tunnel. The others fell in line behind him.

After a minute or so they came to a cavern with a long sloping roof. The high space to their right had been filled with countless chunks of ugly rock, but here and there were broken tools, long since discarded and left to rust.

'We should arm ourselves,' Ash said, raising the torch over the mound of debris.

'What about your club?' Bronwyn asked.

'I'd rather have something a bit . . . pointier.' Ash narrowed his eyes. 'Are you going to tell me where that knife came from?'

Bronwyn began scouring the rubble. 'I found it in one

of the houses in your village.'

'Why didn't you tell me about it?'

Bronwyn shrugged. 'For all I knew then, I might have had to use it on you.'

Ash shook his head. Bronwyn finished selecting a pole: it was as tall as she was and tapered to a blunt point at one end. She picked up another that was almost identical and tossed it to Ash.

'I would've thought you'd be happy about it.'

'Why?'

'It would have come in handy if Vivienne had turned out to be untrustworthy. Or if that dog had come back in the night. And we wouldn't have freed Samuel without it.'

Samuel looked up from the crate he was rummaging through. The smile on his face appeared to be permanent. 'Can we take this?' he said, holding up a pale brick.

'What is it?' Ash said.

Samuel lifted it up to his nose and sniffed. 'I think it's some kind of cake.'

Something echoed in the tunnel at the other end of the cavern. Ash swung around with the torch held high. The tunnel was low, dark and empty.

'Probably just a rock coming loose,' Bronwyn said,

but she didn't sound sure. 'We should keep moving: the sooner we're out of here, the better.'

'Well, can I?' Samuel asked. He was still holding the pale brick.

'Okay,' Ash said, distractedly. He held his satchel open and Samuel rushed over to drop it in. 'Have you got a weapon?'

Samuel lifted his right hand to reveal a long, rusty pole.

'Good. Now, let's go.'

They strode into the tunnel that led deeper into the mountain. It twisted more than the first, and its low ceiling forced them to stoop in sections. The air was as frigid as everywhere else. The fingertips that Ash and Bronwyn traced along the walls for balance were soon too numb to feel the jagged stones. Their nails tore, and the pads of their fingers left smears of blood that glistened briefly before being lost to the darkness.

They came to another, much smaller, cavern. Three passages led from it. At its centre was a small puddle of water, into which a droplet fell from the ceiling every few seconds.

'If we each had a torch we could split up and explore the passages separately,' Bronwyn said.

Ash was very glad they only had one torch. The thought of venturing down one of the tunnels alone sent a violent shudder along his spine.

'Which one should we try first?' Samuel said.

Ash illuminated each of the openings in turn. They all looked alike: dark, jagged, narrow. Ash noticed how the light made the shadowy recesses seem even darker. It also stopped his eyes from adjusting to the gloom, so that everything beyond the circle of orange light took on a blackness so deep it felt infinite.

'We'll try the one on the left,' Ash said, coming to a sudden decision.

He stepped around the little pool and entered the tunnel with Bronwyn and Samuel close behind. They had walked for what felt like hours, although it couldn't have been more than a few minutes, when they came to another tunnel that branched off their own. Ash glanced along it before carrying on. 'We'll stick to this one for now. We can explore that one on the way back if we hit a dead end.'

They went on. The walls became slick with water that collected in puddles in the sunken parts of the path. Abruptly, the path ended. Ash swore.

'Dead end. Turn back.'

The passage was too narrow for Ash to move to the front of the line, and so the torch was passed from Ash to Bronwyn to Samuel. They went back. The constantly shifting bars of darkness tricked Ash's eyes. Shadows became silhouettes.

They reached the corridor that branched off the main tunnel, but it turned out to be little more than a recess.

'Back to the cavern,' Bronwyn whispered.

Samuel led the way. Ash glanced behind and watched the darkness advance along the tunnel as the light moved further away. It seemed to be chasing them – hunting them. He hurried after the silhouettes ahead of him, keeping low and moving as quickly as he dared. Just as Bronwyn was once again within touching distance they reached the cavern. The echo of dripping water took on the sound of distant footsteps.

They entered the middle tunnel, which twisted and turned so much it made Ash wonder what the miners had been searching so wildly for. Its meandering course forced him to keep close to Bronwyn, as the torchlight was regularly snuffed out by a tight bend. More than once he nearly tripped her, and more than once she snapped at him to watch where he was going.

The ceiling got gradually lower and lower, forcing

them to stoop, then double over. They turned a corner and the ceiling suddenly met the floor.

It was another dead end.

Ash tried to imagine burrowing this far into a mountain – the tonnage of rock that must have been excavated – for nothing. It was the kind of project that was only conceivable during the Olden Days.

'Why are there so many dead ends?' he asked.

'It was made by people,' Bronwyn said. 'Dead ends are one of the things we're good at. Now, back.'

The tunnel was too low and narrow to pass the torch, and so Ash was forced to lead the way into a forest of shadows. He took the first steps around a sharp corner in total darkness. He couldn't even be sure that there was rock waiting beneath his outstretched boots. Each step jangled his nerves, and beads of cold sweat began to scurry beneath his tunic.

Finally, he emerged into the small cavern. His hands were trembling, and bands of white and black danced across his vision. He bent over, placing his hands on his knees, and drew deep, icy breaths into his lungs. His breathing was so loud and ragged that it echoed around the chamber. He gulped down a breath and held it in his lungs.

The sound of breathing continued.

Only it wasn't an echo.

He looked up just as Samuel's torch began to illuminate the cavern. There, squatting by the pool, was something. Its grubby skin camouflaged it against the rocks, but its large eyes shone in the brightening chamber. Rags hung from its bony frame. It opened its mouth, revealing sharp little teeth, and emitted a sound that fell somewhere between a cackle and a shriek. It was a guttural, animal sound.

And it wasn't intended for Ash.

The passageway opposite began to echo with a cacophony of evil sounds: scraping, banging, screeching. But loudest of all was an unnerving, hacking laughter that made the cavern feel ten degrees colder.

Ash became aware of Bronwyn and Samuel standing beside him. They too were paralysed by the creature in front of them, which now straightened its skinny, sinewy legs to stand. It must have been taller than any of them, but its upper back and neck were hunched, forcing it to twist its head awkwardly just to look forwards.

In its right hand, clutched within a calloused fist, was a shard of rock. It licked its lips with a pink tongue. And Ash realised, with a sudden retch of horror, that he wasn't looking at a monster. It was far more terrifying than that.

He was looking at a man.

The racket in the tunnel grew louder and louder until it seemed sure to bring the roof crashing down. Samuel's hands hung by his sides, the torch casting a ghoulish light on everything. Bronwyn gave Ash a gentle nudge and glanced meaningfully at the torch. Ash nodded his understanding.

They were still clutching the makeshift weapons they had found in the first cavern, but they suddenly felt useless. The clamour coming from the passage was almost deafening. As soon as the first spectral shapes materialised in the gloom, Bronwyn shouted, 'Now!'

Ash grabbed Samuel's hand and lifted the torch so that it shone full in the face of the person by the pool. He yelped and recoiled, as did the teeming horde emerging from the tunnel behind him, giving them the split second they needed to disappear into the third tunnel.

Samuel went first, followed by Bronwyn. Ash brought up the rear.

'Run!' he shouted.

Harsh sounds bounced around the tunnel. Dark shapes lumbered and scampered through the gloom.

The grunts moved closer – excited, hungry. A cold, clammy hand made a grab for the back of Ash's shirt. He felt the groping fingers like a bolt of lightning and they propelled him forwards. The wet walls of the passage glimmered in the faint light, but Ash knew he was at risk of losing the beacon. If Samuel got too far ahead, his hopes of finding a way out would fade with the light.

He had to run for his life.

The tunnel was straight for long sections, meaning that Ash could keep Samuel and Bronwyn in view as he sprinted after them. But whenever the passage turned, Ash found himself running with little more than hope to guide him. And, all the while, eager grunts and huffs chased him down. Weapons, dull and heavy, knocked against the walls. It was impossible to tell how far behind him they were.

He thought of those grey, grasping fingers and found a new burst of speed.

Ash rounded a corner and regained sight of Samuel. The gap was closing. He pushed on, fighting hard to ignore the stinging ache in his thighs. The noise behind him intensified: whooping and cackling mixed with panting and wheezing.

They were getting closer.

Dark gaps appeared in the walls on either side; passages that led to passages that led to passages. Any one of them might lead to the outside, to daylight and fresh air. Any one of them might lead to a dead end. But Samuel kept to the same tunnel, and Ash had no choice but to follow him.

A cool breeze began to blow hard into Ash's face, pushing him back. He knew he was slowing, even as the gap to Samuel and Bronwyn closed: they were tiring too. The riotous howling amplified until it seemed on the brink of consuming them. Their ears rang with the greedy sounds. Their skulls became miniature caverns, infested with rampaging demons.

Again, Ash thought of the icy fingers, the sharp little teeth in pink gums. His muscles strained for fresh speed but found only biting acid. The familiar feeling of uselessness, of defeat, began to dig its little claws into his flesh.

I am going to stop.

I am going to fail.

I am going to die.

And then new light began to illuminate the tunnel. Ash glanced beyond Samuel and saw parallel grooves worn into the ground. And at the end of them, an opening. The outside. They were nearing an exit! The cold breeze stiffened, as though trying to force him back into the mountain. His eyes watered, forcing him to squint.

He didn't see the jagged knuckle of rock poking from the ceiling.

It caught his skull with enough force to whip his head back. His teeth clacked with sickening violence. He stumbled on under his own momentum, but already his balance was betraying him. He slumped against a wall, clawed his way along it. Something hot dribbled over his forehead. The exit was just steps away – he could feel the sun's heat – but so was the chasing horde. He took another step, and it was as though the muscles in his legs had turned to water. He collapsed and rolled on to his back.

He groaned.

His vision blurred and fizzed with bright colours.

A pair of hands grabbed him.

His eyes fluttered.

And then the hands began to drag him away.

Into darkness.

13

Ash gasped, sitting up as though ejected from a nightmare.

'*Finally*,' Bronwyn said. 'I was beginning to think you weren't coming back.'

Ash choked on the breath he'd inhaled. It tasted of blood and dust. When he'd recovered, he looked around. He was on the Pikes, surrounded by skeletal trees. The dying sun flooded the slope with golden light. Further up was a black hole in the mountainside. From it, something had been dragged, gouging a shallow, blood-spattered channel in the dusty gravel.

Ash did not need to be told what had been dragged. The back of his body felt raw and his head throbbed with every heartbeat. He reached up a tentative hand, working his way through sticky, gritty hair. When he lowered it, his fingers were rosy with blood.

'You bled a bit,' Samuel said, 'but I think I managed

to patch you up all right.'

Ash was still staring at his bloody fingers. Their flight from the passage was coming back to him in fragments: Samuel's silhouette up ahead, and behind . . .

He shivered. 'How long have I been out?'

Samuel shrugged happily. 'I've never been good with time. Maybe you could teach me!'

'An hour,' Bronwyn said. 'Maybe longer.'

Ash shook his head. He stood up and quickly fell to one knee. He squeezed two handfuls of stones.

'Here,' Bronwyn said, bending down to offer him the waterskin. 'Drink.'

Ash was devilishly thirsty. He gulped the water down. It was still chilled from its time inside the mountain.

'More,' Bronwyn said, but Ash shook his head.

'We need to ration it.' He glanced around at the dead trees. 'Where are we?'

'On the northern side of the Pikes,' Samuel said.

'We're through?'

Samuel nodded enthusiastically.

'But we should make a move as soon as possible,' Bronwyn said. 'They might come after us when it gets dark.'

Ash nodded. Bronwyn and Samuel helped him to his

feet. After a moment of dizziness his vision cleared, and he thought he would be able to manage the descent through the forest. He picked up his pole and leaned heavily on it.

'Where are you two going?' Samuel asked. And then, before either of them could answer, he added: 'Can I come too?'

Ash laughed and winced. It felt like a pickaxe had been lodged in the top of his skull. 'We're going to the Kingdom,' he said.

'Ever heard of it?' Bronwyn asked, shooting a wry glance at Ash.

'Of course!'

Bronwyn raised her eyebrows. 'It's real?'

Samuel nodded. 'I've never been there but I've seen it. Do you think they'll let us in?'

'Yes,' Ash said.

But what if they don't? he thought. *What if I was left behind for a reason?*

He pushed the thought away. The Ancestors would not have let him get this far if that were true. He would have starved at the bottom of Vivienne's pit, or been torn apart by that crazed dog, or clubbed to death in the mines, had the Ancestors intended him to fail. But he *had* made it this far, and now the Kingdom was tantalisingly close.

Samuel was bounding around like a lamb at the prospect. Ash would have done the same had he been up to it. The thought of trekking so far, enduring so much, only to be met by disappointment would have crushed his spirit. Instead, relief and delight flooded through him, giving him the strength to go on.

'Where is your family?' Bronwyn asked. 'Your village?'

Samuel's frolicking came to a sudden stop. 'I don't have a village. I've been on my own for as long as I can remember.' He caught sight of Bronwyn's concerned expression. 'Don't worry. I don't do so bad. And now I've got you two and we're going to the Kingdom!'

He suddenly took off down the slope, little shards of rock cascading around him. He stopped as soon as he realised that he was alone. 'You coming or what?' he called. 'You've got to take it at a run – there's no other way.' Then he set off again, the avalanche of stones churning up a cloud of dust in his wake.

'He's odd,' Bronwyn said.

Ash nodded. 'There's no meanness in him. Maybe that comes later, when you've had time for bad things to happen?'

'We found him tied to a rock, moments away from becoming a human sacrifice. If that's not a bad thing, I'm not sure what is.'

'Hurry up!' came the small voice. Samuel was no longer visible.

Ash squinted into the sun's glare. The coolness of the mine was already a distant memory.

'He thinks this is a game,' Bronwyn said. 'When do you think he'll realise that it's not?'

Ash shook his head. 'I don't know. But it's kind of nice, isn't it? I think we should make sure he doesn't grow up. At least not while he's with us.'

'Agreed.'

Ash and Bronwyn raced each other down the hillside, tiny rocks bouncing and tinkling around them. For a few minutes, they were both reminded of what it was like to be a child. Ash remembered – for the first time in many years – running down the slopes of Last Village with his father, the sheep bounding out of their way, while his mother watched on from beneath the shade of a tree that had since been uprooted by a storm. It was almost possible, as he ran ahead of Bronwyn, to imagine that his father was here now, chasing after him while his mother looked on from beneath that long-dead tree.

Almost.

They hurtled down the long slope, carried by their own momentum, kept upright by a need to preserve this rare moment of happy exhilaration. It felt wonderful to be running for the thrill of it, rather than for their lives. To forget about the scarcity of water was as good as drinking the stuff itself. To make a breeze on a still day filled them with a sense of power they had rarely ever known. They ran because it felt good to run.

They saw Samuel in a clearing, smiling broadly at the pleasure and pandemonium he had caused. The slope levelled out: loose stones turned to dry earth. Ash and Bronwyn came to a stop on either side of Samuel and rested with their hands on their knees. They drew deep breaths that stung their lungs. The top of Ash's head pounded and tingled. The late sun beat down on them, punishing them for their recklessness. Sweat dripped from their noses and left dark pockmarks in the dust.

'Good, eh?' Samuel said. 'Want to go back up and do it again?'

Ash smiled and looked up, but what he saw beyond Samuel's shoulder wiped the smile from his face. At the edge of the clearing the ground fell away to reveal a large plain, bisected by a stream. Its grass was green – a deep, luscious emerald – and the water caught the late light and burned orange. Ash followed its winding course with his eyes, and it led him to something that made him fall to his knees as though confronted by the Four Fathers themselves.

On the far side of the plain, a mile or more away, two hills rose on either side of the stream, leaning away from one another to create a narrow valley. In the gap between them a huge stone wall had been constructed: three hundred feet high at least, its sandy-coloured blocks shining gold in the sunlight.

'What is that?' Bronwyn asked.

'The Kingdom,' Ash said, for if there was ever a place the Four Fathers called home, this was it.

'That's not the Kingdom,' Samuel said. 'That's the Wall.'

Ash turned his head sharply. 'The Wall?'

Samuel picked at a scab on his knee with determined interest. 'Yep. The Kingdom's further north. You can see it from up there, though.' He neglected his knees for long enough to point out the long line of hills on either side of the Wall.

But it was the Wall that held Ash's attention.

It was the largest built thing he had ever seen. He

would not have thought such wonders possible just moments earlier. It made him feel smaller than he already knew himself to be. It could only have been built by the Four Fathers, and he said as much aloud.

'Don't be daft,' Samuel said, addressing his knees once more. ''Twas made by people.'

'The Four Fathers *were* people,' Ash said, 'before they ascended and became gods.'

Samuel shrugged. 'You know more about that than me, I suppose, but I'm telling you it weren't there when I was little. Well, littler than I am now. It was built by people. And I can prove it.'

Bronwyn arched an eyebrow. 'How?'

'Follow me and I'll show you.'

They set off again, the brittle trees creaking in the heat. The forest floor was dusty and scarred by roots that groped for water – in vain. The last leaves had fallen many years before, and had long since been swept away by ferocious, scouring winds. The branches that remained cast thick, stumpy shadows on the ground.

'What do your gods look like?' Samuel asked. The pole he carried was taller than him, and he had taken to planting it in the dusty ground and swinging himself forward.

'They're your gods, too,' Ash said.

'Are they big?'

'Nobody knows what they look like,' Ash said. 'They lived a long time ago. But they have the power to stir up a storm, or to bring a flood, or to hide the sun.' He pointed at the Wall, shining through the empty canopy. 'They could tear down that wall in a moment.'

Samuel's eyes were wide. 'They're the ones that hid the sun?'

'That's right.'

Bronwyn tutted, but Samuel let out an appreciative whistle. Then he stopped abruptly and leaned on his pole. 'Hang on. If they can hide the sun, why do they let it burn us? Don't they like us?' Samuel looked crestfallen; no sooner had he acquired some gods to worship than he discovered they might hate him.

Ash spoke slowly, choosing his words carefully. He wished Helena were there; she always knew how to speak about the Four Fathers. 'They do like us, Samuel, very much. We are their family, after all. But they make us suffer to bring out our true nature.' He recalled something Helena had once said and quickly repeated it. 'The sun burns, but it also illuminates.'

'What is ill-oom-in-ates?'

Ash's heart sank. The proverb had seemed so elegant – made so much sense – coming from Helena's lips. He was sure he would only mangle it further in the explanation. Bronwyn saw his disappointment and took pity.

'It means making something light that would otherwise be dark. Ash is saying that the sun is both a good thing and a bad thing, and he believes that the gods made it that way to bring out the good and bad in us.'

Samuel's face lit up. 'So if I'm good, the gods will like me?'

'That's right,' said Ash.

Samuel set off again, swinging on his pole with renewed energy. 'That's all right then. I'll just be good. Being good is easy.'

Ash and Bronwyn exchanged a glance, and Ash mouthed, 'Thank you.'

They stepped around a large tree trunk that lay across their path (Samuel vaulted over it on the third attempt) and continued down the barren slope.

Samuel wanted to know everything there was to know about the Four Fathers. 'What happens if you're bad?'

'If you're bad, the Four Fathers won't forgive you. They'll make you suffer in this life and the next.'

Samuel's mouth dropped open. 'There's another life after this one?'

'Yes.'

'What's it like?'

'It's like living in the world as it used to be, back in the Olden Days. There's plenty of water to go around, the sun isn't so hot, and the trees are green.'

'*Green?* Are you sure? That doesn't sound right.' Samuel looked mistrustfully at the withered trunks around him.

'Yes. There are lots more animals, too.'

Samuel shrugged at that. 'I'm not sure whether more animals would be such a good thing. Sheep have their uses, but what's the point in more rats and mozzies and roaches?'

Ash laughed. It was fun to share a picture of a better world, especially with someone who seemed as excited about it as he did.

'Not just more of the animals we already have; in the next life, there are hundreds of different types – ones we can't even imagine. An *abundance*, the Priestess in my village called it.'

Samuel frowned and opened his mouth, but Ash pre-empted the question: 'An abundance means a lot.'

Satisfied, Samuel listened as Ash tried to describe some of the creatures he had witnessed in the crinkly yellow pages of Helena's books – animals that soared and swam, scurried and stalked: eagles and parrots and bats and whales and dolphins and sharks and hedgehogs and deer and unicorns and wolves and lions and tigers. A thousand types of fish. Bears big enough to eat a man in one sitting. Slithery things that came without legs. Horses that came with four. Tiny critters that came with six, eight, a hundred.

It was too good to believe. It was too good to disbelieve.

'And they all used to be real?' Samuel asked. 'You're not joshing me?'

Ash nodded solemnly. Samuel whistled. Bronwyn held her tongue. They were quiet for a long time. Finally, Samuel spoke.

'How do you get to the next life? Do you have to die?'

Ash shook his head. 'No. You can be called to the Kingdom by the Four Fathers, like my village was. One day, the Four Fathers will remake the world as it was, when we have atoned for our sins. But till then we must do our best in this life, and look forward to the next.'

They were nearing the edge of the forest. The trees

here had borne the brunt of a thousand storms, and most lay branchless and broken on the ground. Their stumps stood like squat tombstones, and the sky above them was large. Before they emerged from the forest, Samuel stopped in the shade of one of the few remaining trees. It had lost all its branches. It looked like a lonely soldier after a battlefield massacre.

'Why did all the animals go away in the first place?' Samuel asked.

'I don't know,' Ash said, gazing out at the grassy plain. 'But it was all our fault.'

Samuel nodded slowly, as though he'd assumed as much. Then the cheer returned to his features, and he set out across the plain at a skip. 'Almost there now,' he called. 'Keep up.'

The plain was about a mile wide, and with every step the Wall loomed higher, as though it were pushing upwards like a tooth from a gum. It was all Ash and Bronwyn could look at, but Samuel did not seem particularly interested by it. They followed the stream for a short time – its steep banks suggesting that it had once been a mighty torrent – before cutting across the meadow, towards the hills to the right of the Wall.

Ash was glad. To approach the Wall directly felt

unwise – blasphemous, even. He could not look at it without thinking of the Four Fathers, and he was not prepared to meet the Four Fathers yet. Not after what had happened to Helena.

A small settlement came into view at the foot of the Wall. It sat like a dirty smudge on the hem of a golden gown.

'Who lives there?' Bronwyn asked.

Samuel shrugged without looking around. 'I don't know. People, is all I know. And I keep myself away from people if I can. They're not to be trusted.'

Bronwyn frowned. The words were at odds with Samuel's childish exuberance, but when he glanced back there was a wide smile on his face once more.

'Except you two, of course. I can trust you.'

The Wall did not become any less imposing when viewed from the side. They could see now that it was made from hundreds of huge stone blocks. On the far side, a series of ropes stretched the full height of the Wall.

'What is it for?' Ash said.

'To keep things in,' Samuel said. 'What else are walls for?'

'To keep things out?' Bronwyn suggested.

Samuel stopped at the foot of the hill and scratched his head. 'Oh, yeah.'

'What does it keep in?' Ash said.

'You'll see.'

They began to climb. It was so steep that they had to zigzag upwards, keeping one hand close to the sloping earth. The emerald turf was deep and springy, the soil beneath it dark and damp. Little crumbs of dirt clung to their fingertips, carrying a scent that was as rich as blood. Here and there, shy flowers grew close to the ground.

As they neared the peak the ground turned rocky: big, rounded humps of stone mottled with pale lichen. Little lumps and indents served as handholds, and with a final effort the three children hauled themselves on to the summit.

Countless years of wind and rain had worn the top of the hill smooth. Small boulders lay scattered about as though the gods had abandoned a game of marbles. Off to the right, two huge slabs of rock overlapped to form a low cave.

But it was what lay on the other side – to the west – that caught Ash and Bronwyn's attention. The hill fell away sharply, down towards the top of the Wall, and they saw then what lay behind it: the thing that it kept in.

'Water,' Bronwyn whispered.

Ash shook his head in disbelief. 'The sea.'

And it might have been a sea, for all he knew. A great expanse of water, blue-black and twinkling in the last of the daylight, filled the space between the hills. It stretched so far back that the edge of it was hidden behind a lower peak.

'It's not a sea,' Samuel said. 'It's a lake. A reservoir.'

Ash followed its glistening surface as far as he could with his eyes, before letting them drift over the hills rising and falling to the north. In the far distance, something else shimmered. It shone like a diamond waiting to be prised from the earth.

'What is that?' Ash said.

Samuel answered without taking his eyes from the water.

'That's the Kingdom,' he said. 'And this is what they drink.'

Ash squinted at the domed and distant jewel. For so long he had imagined such a place, prayed to be taken there, doubted its existence in a hundred moments of despair. And there it was, dazzling and indistinct – but there. Real.

Four Fathers be praised.

Ash fell to his knees and tilted his face to the sky. At this hour and altitude the sun held his cheek like a soft hand, cast the hills in a patchwork of ever-darkening greens, transformed the lake into a rucked rug of woven light. It *illuminated*, when for so long it had burned. He felt closer to the Four Fathers than at any other point in his life. He saw now why he had suffered for so long. Why, even, Helena had been taken.

'Wait.'

It was Bronwyn. He looked to her in irritation. She had not fallen to her knees, as she should have. She had not even noticed his rapture. She was looking at the lake – no, the Wall – pointing. 'What—?' she said, her eyebrows drawn tightly together.

Ash had to stand to see. He clambered to his feet and stood beside her. They looked down the hillside, to the barrier of golden stone. Along its top, small but unmistakable, people moved back and forth. At the far end a platform rose to meet the Wall, hoisted up on hanging ropes, and a huge stone block was manoeuvred out on a wheeled cart.

They watched as the giant stone was dragged along the top of the Wall – dragged by a team of ten men wearing yolks and harnesses. The men's torsos were angled low, and their effort was obvious despite the slowness of the cart. Ash and Bronwyn scanned the Wall and saw another team – children, they seemed to be – filling pails at a trough and emptying them into a large cavity in the Wall. Another group of children trampled through the beige muck, their smocks clutched up above their knees. Beside the pit, another team made adjustments to a timber contraption festooned with rope.

'It weren't made by no gods,' Samuel said, as Ash and Bronwyn looked on, their mouths working but forming no sounds. 'It were made by people. And they ain't finished yet.'

Ash watched as the stone block made its way along the Wall. When it finally reached the cavity, the pulling team unburdened themselves and the team by the contraption began to loop ropes around the giant block. The children climbed out of the hole and lifted up the ladders behind them. Slowly, the block began to rise. It was guided over the cavity and then began to descend. The teams called to one another: regular, reassuring noises, as though they were herding sheep into a pen.

Ash looked to Samuel. 'Who are those people? Where did they come from?'

But he knew, just as Bronwyn knew. Before Samuel could answer, a rope snapped and the block dipped low on one side. One of the men who had hauled it – short but stocky, his beard black – called out, and his voice carried clearly to the hilltop.

'Watch it, boy!'

Ash recognised the voice. Recognised, above all, the final word: *boy*.

'Dain,' he whispered. His eyes scanned the workers. There were many he couldn't place, but there were plenty that he could. The children tasked with carrying and stirring the mortar all looked alike: even at this distance, the way they stood at the edge of the cavity was familiar. They had stood the very same way beside the pool, back in Last Village, clutching rocks while he cleared it for Helena. He saw the straw-like tangle of Tristan's beard, the stooping figure of Kelly the butcher. Beside him, inevitably, stood Loxley the weaver, his short silver hair shining like dull metal. There were others, too, that Bronwyn clearly recognised from her own village; she stood with her hand over her mouth, her eyes wide.

Further along the Wall there were more teams completing other tasks, but they were too distant to identify – too many to be just the people from Ash and Bronwyn's villages. Along the inside of the Wall, suspended above the water, were little shacks with boardwalks between them. Their roofs were thick with mortar that had oozed from between the blocks and landed in ugly splats.

And all along the Wall, men in peculiar wide-brimmed hats stood by, watching. They each carried something curved and vicious. Something that caught the sunlight and shone like lightning.

The trail of abandoned villages was a mystery no longer. Their inhabitants had not been called into a new life of peace and prosperity by the Four Fathers; they had been kidnapped and forced to build a giant wall by men with glowing blades of death on their hips.

For the first time in his life, Ash feared something more than the Four Fathers.

He fell to his knees once more.

14

'We have to help them,' Bronwyn said.

Samuel looked as though she had suggested eating the boulders around her feet. 'Don't you see the guards?'

'I don't care about the guards! We have to help them.'

Samuel looked at Ash, who knelt with his head hanging low. 'Are you okay?'

Ash shook his head. Just a few minutes before, when he knelt in reverence of the Four Fathers, he hadn't been able to feel the rock beneath his knees. Now, it pressed against his kneecaps with excruciating force. And yet he could not face the climb to his feet.

'I don't understand,' he muttered, addressing the ground. 'This can't be it. I thought we'd made it. I thought—'

A pair of hands grabbed his shirt and hauled him to his feet. Bronwyn stared hard into his face. 'When are you going to accept that we're alone? There are no gods!

Our ancestors don't care about us! They're dead! They created this world and left us to suffer in it!' She took a deep breath and pressed her lips into a thin line. 'Nobody is coming to save you. You have to save yourself.'

Ash nodded in a daze. His eyes slid from Bronwyn's face and drifted to the Kingdom, dazzling in the distance. The setting sun had transformed it from a diamond to a lump of amber. 'But—'

Bronwyn shook him. Her voice was soft now, and it was harder to ignore than any shout. 'If you want us to survive, and if you want to help those people down there, you have to let your gods go. Do you understand?'

Ash swallowed. Eventually he nodded. Bronwyn released her grip.

'Okay then.' She breathed deeply. 'It's just me and you now.'

Ash nodded again.

'What about me?' Samuel said.

Bronwyn closed her eyes and a small smile flickered at the corner of her lips. 'Okay. It's just me and you and him.'

Samuel beamed. 'Great! Now, come on. We can rest in the cave. I've got a couple of fleece blankies tucked away.'

Bronwyn collected their satchels and poles and carried them to the cave. Ash stood alone for a while, a gentle breeze blowing his hair about his face. Through a tangle of dark strands, he watched the Kingdom transform from a piece of amber into a glistening ruby. The hills around it darkened, and by the time Ash finally turned away, it glowed like the eye of some shadowy beast.

He found Bronwyn and Samuel sitting on dirty swathes of wool. As Ash ducked beneath the entrance to the cave, Bronwyn scooted along and offered him a strip of cured mutton. He took it and sat down. He tore a piece off with his teeth and chewed, while Bronwyn resumed her conversation with Samuel.

'What I don't understand is how the Wall got so high so fast. The people in my village went missing less than a week ago, and the stream dried up just a few days ago. How is that possible?'

Samuel licked the white brick he had found in the mines and clearly decided that it was not some kind of cake. He sampled some dried berries instead. His mouth was full but that didn't stop him from replying. 'They started building the Wall years ago. It must have taken ages to cut the stone and bring it here, and obviously you can't build in the middle of a river.' He stopped to spit out a little black seed. 'They had to redirect it while they built the lower part of the Wall, which is why your stream didn't dry up years ago. It was only recently that it got high enough to block the new course and return it to the old one.'

'Which is now blocked by the Wall?'

Samuel nodded. Bronwyn took a sip of water and passed the skin to Ash. He waved it away. Samuel reached out and took a thirsty swig.

'If the Wall is trapping all the water from the river,' Bronwyn asked, 'won't it eventually spill over the top?' It was difficult enough to imagine the Wall was real, now that it was out of sight and shrouded in darkness. But to imagine even *more* water – enough to overwhelm such a colossal structure – was close to impossible.

Samuel chewed on a mutton strip. 'There's a place on the far side that lets the water escape when it reaches a certain level. They'll block that when the Wall is higher.' He tore off another piece. 'There's a tunnel to the Kingdom, too – a pipe. Runs through the hills. Takes the water straight to them.'

The idea of a pipe that brought water – as much as

you could ever want – straight to your cup was dizzying. *A godlike luxury*, Ash thought, but he said nothing.

'Who lives in the Kingdom?' Bronwyn asked.

Just a few hours earlier, Ash would have jumped in to answer. He would have told her the Kingdom was the place the saved were taken to when their penance had been paid. The dwelling of the Four Fathers, and all their favoured descendants. And, although he might not have convinced Bronwyn, he would have convinced and reassured himself. Now, he was glad of the chewy meat that snagged between his teeth. He had nothing left to say.

Samuel shrugged. 'No idea. Never been that far north. All I know is that they got the know-how to build the biggest wall I've ever seen. To make a lake. They must be powerful folk. Mighty folk. Kings, I've heard 'em called.'

Bronwyn shook her head, in anger and despair. 'How do we help them?'

Ash scowled. 'The Kings?'

'No! Those people down there. *Our* people.'

Ash realised he had barely spared a thought for the people of Last Village and felt ashamed. It was that kind of selfishness that incurred the wrath of the Four Fathers.

But what did that matter now? If Bronwyn was right, their wrath was constant: a jagged boulder that had been pushed down a bottomless hill, wrecking everything in its path. *For ever and ever. Amen.* They would punish him if he did something, and they would punish him if he did nothing.

And still. The thought of turning his back on his people just would not stick. They would expect that of him, what with him being his father's son, and although it was tempting to prove them right just to spite them, he couldn't bring himself to suggest it. He had needed them in the past, and they had failed him. They needed him now, and he would not fail them.

'Bronwyn's right. We have to help.'

Samuel stared at him in amazement. 'I think that bump on the head was worse than we thought.' He looked to Bronwyn. 'I don't know what your excuse is.'

'How many guards are there on the Wall?' Ash said.

Samuel shrugged. 'Never been much good at counting, but I know for sure there's more of them than there is of you.'

'Us,' Bronwyn said. 'Remember?'

Samuel smiled. 'Of course! There's more of them than there is of us. And they come with swords.'

'There must be a time when the Wall is unguarded?' Ash said.

Samuel scratched his head. 'Can't say I ever saw it unguarded. The workers sleep in those shacks at night. They're not allowed off the Wall. And there's guards on the Wall all night. Not so many, because most of them goes down to the settlement. But still more than one-two-three.'

Ash looked at Bronwyn, and they both felt the prickle of powerlessness.

'Is it safe up here?' Bronwyn asked.

'Nobody ever came here but me. Safe as Sam.'

'What are you thinking?' Ash asked Bronwyn.

'We could stay up here for a few days and watch the Wall. There must be a way to get a message to the people there, or a time when the guards are less alert.'

'The Kings pay them well to stay awake,' Samuel said. 'But I don't know if anyone's ever tried to get on the Wall. Most people want to get off it.'

Ash nodded. 'So we watch and we wait and we pray' – he caught himself, cleared his throat – '*hope* for an opportunity.'

Bronwyn nodded. 'Do you mind if we stay here, Samuel?'

Samuel was busy picking a piece of mutton from between his teeth. He stopped and wiped his fingers on his thigh. He beamed.

'Not at all,' he said. 'You can stay for ever. We're a family now, remember?'

15

Ash dreamed of water, a whole lake of it. He stood on the shore, watching little ripples wash over his toes. And then, in the way of dreams, he was drowning. He thrashed in a swarm of bubbles. He kicked, straining for the surface, but the twinkling canopy remained just beyond his reach. He heard voices, muffled by the water, and knew they spoke of him.

'How many?'

'Two.'

'Just two?'

'No. Two. There en't no "just" about it.'

'Children?'

'Just about. Bigger than me, smaller than you.'

'Are they fit to work?'

'Course. Trekked all the way here from Last Village. The girl's tough. She keeps a knife tucked in her boot.'

'And what about the boy?'

'I don't know what to make of him yet.'

'Well, we'll soon find out.'

Ash opened his eyes. The low cave was full of dark shapes. He kicked out and called to Bronwyn but strong hands pinned him to the ground. He was hauled to his feet and dragged outside. Moments later, Bronwyn appeared beside him. One of the men reached down and plucked a knife from inside her boot. He turned it over to someone who stood directly opposite them – a tall, slender man in a wide-brimmed hat, silhouetted against the inky sky. Ash realised with a stab of dread that his club was still in the cave.

'Light,' the man said.

Ash and Bronwyn squinted against the sudden glare of a lantern. By the time they reopened their eyes, the man before them was no longer a silhouette. Golden light fell on the right side of his face, revealing a thin mouth, a straight sharp nose and a beady eye in a sunken socket. He was clean shaven, as were the men holding Ash and Bronwyn, and the sight filled Ash with mistrust: all the men he had ever known had worn beards. The other side of the man's face was cast in shadow, but the light caught the underside of his hat and gave his head an eerie half-substance.

The light also illuminated Samuel – standing, unguarded, off to one side – and Bronwyn made a lunge for him. He flinched, but the men held Bronwyn back. The man with the lantern laughed: a short, bitter sound.

'Ha! You weren't lying about this one, young Samuel. She's got plenty of spirit.' The half-smile fell from his half face. 'We'll break that soon enough.' The dark eye swivelled in its socket and fell upon Ash. It widened ever so slightly – a flash of something resembling recognition – before turning sharp once more. 'And what about you? Do we need to break you as well, or will you come quietly like a good boy?'

Ash did not need to be told who these men were, nor what had happened while he slept: Samuel would not look at him. Fury burned in Ash's chest. He wanted to fight, but he had so little fight left in him. He looked at his captor, bathed in golden light and black shadow, and in that moment he seemed imbued with godly power.

Ash lowered his head. After a moment, he shook it. He could sense the man's smirk, could feel Bronwyn's disappointment.

'Very well,' the man said. 'You may refer to me as the Warden and nothing else. Is that understood?'

Ash and Bronwyn nodded, but the Warden waited expectantly.

'Yes, Warden,' they mumbled.

'Very good. Now, let's go.'

The Warden turned away, and his men shoved Ash and Bronwyn after him. They had barely taken a step when Samuel spoke up.

'What about my payment?'

The Warden stopped and looked over his shoulder. He seemed to be appraising Samuel, deciding something. A change came over Samuel's face: his pout slackened, his scowling eyes grew wide. But then the Warden nodded, and one of the others took a sack from his belt and held it out. Samuel snatched it and peered inside. Then he swung it over his shoulder and fled into the darkness.

The party set off once more and Ash staggered forwards under the force of another shove. He wanted to know, more than anything, what was in that sack. He was desperate to learn what Samuel had traded his and Bronwyn's freedom for. He knew now that Samuel had been seeing his prize whenever he looked at his new companions. But what was it? What price did two lost children fetch in this endlessly cruel world? Whatever it was, it was small enough to fit into a bag the size of a stomach, and light enough to be thrown over a bony shoulder and carried away.

The question infuriated him. He was certain it would plague his thoughts and haunt his dreams.

But he would forget about Samuel soon enough: he suspected worse things waited on the Wall.

It took longer to reach the Wall than seemed possible, but its size disguised its distance. Down and ever down, the men and their captives plodded. The sky was beginning to pale with the first light of dawn by the time they arrived. The blades of the waiting guards shone glossy and pink. They all wore the same wide-brimmed hats, and their shirts and trousers were made of a material that was thinner than anything Loxley had ever managed to weave. On their feet they wore boots, but the leather was dark and not at all like sheepskin.

The guards at the edge of the Wall stepped aside as the group approached, bestowing little more than a cursory glance on the new arrivals. Ash and Bronwyn passed a weatherworn gatehouse and took their first step on to the Wall just as the sun peeked above the horizon. Their shadows stretched out ahead of them, all the way to the opposite hill. The vast expanse of water lay to their right like some sort of miracle, and they could almost feel the weight of it, straining to break free from its confinement. On the other side, the plains stretched away to the desiccated forest and jagged peaks of the Pikes.

They passed the section of the Wall they had watched being built the previous day, coming to a place where the huge blocks were twice as wide and formed a complete path. The Warden stopped at a wooden post in the middle of the Wall. He grasped a rope that hung from a bell. He paused, seeming to savour the silence of the dawn. Then he rang the bell with a vicious snap of his wrist. The clanging sound ripped through the air, filling it like a headache.

Ash and Bronwyn looked along the Wall, waiting. For a few moments, nothing happened. And then, people began to appear all along the right-hand side. They clambered up ladders that dangled over the water, like rats emerging from their burrows, and congregated in a semicircle around the Warden. They moved quickly and silently, and took up their positions as though they were marked out on the blocks beneath their feet. Ash recognised many people from his village, but there were many more who were strangers from strange places. Ash glanced from face to face. The people stood like a defeated army. There was no warmth, no interest: only fatigue and pain and resentment. Most of them focused on the Warden. The ones that watched Ash and Bronwyn did so with eyes that were sharp with scorn and dull with defeat.

We must remind them of what they've lost, Ash thought. *What we've all lost.*

The Warden released the rope and placed his hands on his hips. 'Today is a good day,' he said, and the words hit Ash like a fist in the gut. 'You have two new recruits to lighten your load.' He held out a hand, directing the sullen attention of the crowd to Ash and Bronwyn. The sun was at his back, but Ash felt his cheeks burn.

'This is a place of rules and discipline,' the Warden announced. 'Follow the rules, work hard, and you will enjoy a pleasant life here. Not an easy life: no one is promising you that. But a life in which your hard work is rewarded.'

He looked out across the glittering water. The crowd squinted into the rising sun, and their faces told Ash just how hard his life would be. He noticed, amongst the frowns, one man staring at him with particular intent.

The man's bald head shone, and his dark skin was criss-crossed with pale scars. He scowled at Ash as though he were an enemy long presumed dead. Ash looked away, towards the reservoir, but every time he glanced back he found the man watching.

'This water belongs to the Kingdom – all of it – and it is only by the grace of the Kings that you are permitted to drink it. You may dip your pitcher in the barrels along the Wall once in the morning, once at midday, and once in the evening. Anyone caught pilfering will be given more water than they could ever hope to drink.'

The surface twinkled benignly, but the Warden's meaning was clear.

'There will be no fighting amongst you. Each of you is the property of the Kings – any damage you inflict on another will have to be compensated.' A cruel smile commandeered his face. 'That being said, the overseers and I are at liberty to dispose of any . . . defective workers. No one leaves the Wall without my express permission. Anyone caught trying will be shown the fastest route down.'

The Warden's eyes were fixed in a permanent squint, despite the deep shade cast by his hat, and his narrow eyes slid towards the opposite side of the Wall. The others could not help but follow, drawn irresistibly to the site of grisly things by some preserving instinct.

'There are bones down there,' the Warden said to Ash and Bronwyn. 'Take a look, if you don't believe me.'

Neither of them moved. Ash was sure the Warden was the type of man to lie about many things, but this was not one of them. Instead, he looked at the expansive view stretching away to the south, Homewards.

'I trust any unacceptable behaviour will be reported to myself or one of my esteemed brethren immediately.' The Warden let these words hang in the air, like a noose waiting for a victim. 'You'll get your meals as they come and you won't ask for more. You'll do the jobs you've been assigned to and won't complain. Your working day is done when there is no light left in the day. Is that understood?'

'Yes, Warden,' the crowd mumbled. To hear them all speak as one, when for so long they had stood in silence, together but seemingly apart, made Ash's scalp prickle. It was eerie, like listening to a gathering of the resurrected dead.

The Warden turned to Ash and Bronwyn and arched a dark eyebrow. 'Is that understood?'

Ash and Bronwyn exchanged an uncertain glance.

Ash could see that Bronwyn was itching to say something unwise, and he gave his head a little shake.

'Yes, Warden,' they said.

'Good.' He clapped his hands together. 'Now, as new arrivals you are entitled to a special treat. Something we call an initiation. A way of becoming part of the community here.'

The guards nearby laughed, and those further along the Wall turned to watch. The crowd shuffled and fidgeted and edged backwards. They knew what was coming and they did not want to be a part of it. Ash felt his empty stomach turn another twist.

He watched the Warden step towards a timber scaffold that jutted out over the water. Ash had not paid it much attention till now, assuming it to be just another pulley or crane that allowed the workers to move the hulking cubes of stone. But he soon realised that he had been mistaken: at the end of a beam, hanging high above the water on a length of rusty chain, was a cage. It swung ever so slightly, screeching in the breeze. It was just a few lengths of metal bolted together, but it wore its menace like a mask.

The Warden reached up and pulled the beam around, bringing the cage to the edge of the Wall. He unclasped the door and turned to face Ash and Bronwyn. For a horrifying moment, Ash thought they were going to be ordered to climb inside. But then the Warden's smile widened, and Ash realised that the punishment was going to be far crueller.

'Pick someone,' he said.

Ash and Bronwyn stared at him.

'Sorry?' Ash said.

'Pick someone.' The Warden tilted his head towards the others. The significance of what they were being asked to do suddenly became apparent.

'No.'

The word was out before Ash could stop it. He clapped a hand to his mouth in a futile attempt to catch it and drag it back. The crowd muttered and shifted. The guards placed their hands on the hilts of their swords.

The Warden cocked an eyebrow. 'No?'

Ash glanced at Bronwyn, and he saw the fear in her eyes.

'What if we don't?' Ash said.

'You must,' came the reply.

'But what if we don't?'

A flutter passed through the crowd. They looked at one another – hopefully, fearfully.

'If you don't, *I* will pick someone. And when that person's turn is over, I will pick someone else. And so on and so forth until everyone here has a reason to hate you.'

Ash knew what it meant to be hated: he had been a pariah for most of his life. And the moment he condemned even one person to this barbaric punishment he would earn everyone's loathing. He would be a perpetrator of their suffering, just like the Warden. Even now, as they waited for him to make his choice, their fear and mistrust of him grew.

But then he had a thought, and he gave it voice before the coward in him had time to smother it.

'Can I choose myself?'

The murmuring crowd fell silent. The Warden eyed Ash like a nail upon which he'd just drawn blood. And again, there was recognition – a question – in his eyes.

'No.'

The murmuring resumed. The Warden silenced it with a look. Ash and Bronwyn exchanged a desperate glance. There seemed to be no way to win. Eventually, they both turned their gaze on the waiting crowd, fearful and fidgety once more. They reminded Ash of Tristan's flock, when he had them corralled in a pen with Kelly the slaughterman standing by.

Ash found himself unable to choose. He knew dozens of the people before him – had been ridiculed and shunned and attacked by many of them – and yet no one deserved this fate. As for the rest: they were strangers, and as strangers he had no reason to trust them, but also no reason to hate them.

Bronwyn seemed to be having the same problem. For a full minute they stood in silence, looking from one blameless face to another. The day grew brighter and hotter. The Warden did not seem to mind that time was wasting. The Wall, it seemed, came second to his sadistic pleasure.

Just when Ash was on the verge of pointing blindly into the crowd, someone spoke up. He recognised the gruff voice instantly, but it was not one that he had expected to hear.

'I'll do it.'

Ash and Bronwyn watched as Dain eased his way through the bodies before him. He crossed his thick arms over his chest and turned to address the Warden. He did not look at Ash or Bronwyn: he did not seem able to.

'I dunno if you heard me, but I said I'll do it.'

The Warden smiled. This was clearly a new way of

playing the game. 'You know what happens next?'

'Course I do.' Dain spat on the ground. 'Same as what happened the day I was brought here. Same as what happens every time one of you lot gets bored.'

The Warden looked amused. 'Then why would you volunteer?'

Dain finally looked at Ash and Bronwyn. 'Because these two are mine. I am responsible for them as an Elder of Last Village. There's only two of us left – after what your lot did to the Priestess – and that tall spindle of a branch back there is hardly going to step forward, is he?'

Dain jabbed a thumb over his shoulder and Ash spotted Tristan, trying to make himself inconspicuous.

The Warden frowned, but a curious smile lingered on his lips. 'That's very noble of you, *Elder*, but I feel obliged to remind you that Last Village no longer exists. It lives on only in your imagination, and soon enough your memories will fade. A year hence, it might never have existed. You are an elder of nowhere, now. Why suffer for something that no longer is?'

'You're right,' Dain said, and the words sent a flash of panic through Ash's chest. 'I'm nothing now. But that don't matter. It's the principle. I wronged the girl, when she first showed up. You can still see the bruising round her eye, if you look close.' Dain did not look close: he looked instead at his hands. 'I shouldn't have done that – shouldn't have called for her banishment.' He looked up again, his expression weary. 'Well, the Four Fathers are punishing me now, that's for sure.'

The Warden looked down on Dain as though he were a foolish child. 'Your gods do not exist any more. They disappeared with your village. The Kings are your gods now.'

Dain set his face into a scowl that Ash had been burned by a hundred times before. In the past, he would have struck a man down for such disrespect. But now he just quivered with rage, and bit his lip, and waited.

'What about the boy?' the Warden said.

Dain looked at Ash, and it took a moment for the scowl to fade. 'I wronged the boy ever since his father . . . Well, ever since he became an orphan. I've never been kind to him – been the opposite, in fact.' He cleared his throat and raised his chin. It did not make him much taller, but he grew in the minds of those watching. 'He can take this as recompense, if he will.'

Ash did not know what to think. For years he had viewed Dain like a feral dog that has gone too long between meals. To see him now – hear his remorse –

made him feel more of a Last Villager than he had ever felt. Now, when he was the furthest from home he had ever been.

The Warden looked at Dain as though he were a new and especially clever type of trap. He smirked. 'Very well,' he said. 'Step up here.'

Dain obeyed without a word. It would have been so easy to push the Warden off the Wall, but Dain obviously knew how foolish a move that would be. It would be the last thing he ever did. Instead, he stepped into the waiting cage and turned to face the others. The door squealed shut. The chain squeaked and the timber arm groaned as it was swung out over the water once more.

The Warden stood beside the crane. There was a short lever at the level of his knee and, after a brief glance at Ash and Bronwyn, he lifted his dark boot and brought it down with a violent stamp. A coil of rope was set loose and the cage – which Ash had expected to hang in the blistering sun for hours – plummeted towards the water below.

He rushed to the edge with Bronwyn and peered over. They were just in time to see an eruption of white water as the cage disappeared beneath the surface. Ash looked at the Warden, who inspected the boot that still rested on the lever, gleaming in the sun.

'We have to do something,' Ash said. 'We have to haul him up!'

'You will do no such thing,' the Warden said, licking the pad of his thumb and rubbing at an imperceptible scuff.

Ash looked to the others. He saw people from Last Village – Quinn and Wren and Kelly and Loxley and Mildred – all looking to the Warden. Waiting.

The Warden stooped closer to his boot, squinted, then leaned back. Finally, he removed his sole from the lever and strode to the southern edge of the Wall. He took off his hat and ran a hand over his close-cropped hair. He watched the Pikes intently, as though they had a habit of changing. Then he replaced the hat on his head and held out a hand. After a moment's hesitation, he twitched his fingers in an upwards direction.

Several people rushed to the crane and began wrestling with the winch. Ash and Bronwyn joined them, and together they wound in the rope. Little splinters pierced the skin of Ash's palms, and his fingers burned against the rough handles, but slowly – inch by inch – the cage began to rise.

When the cage finally reached the arm from which it hung, a few of the villagers held the winch steady while Ash yanked the lever back into place. Quinn reached up and swung the cage in.

Dain coughed and spluttered, water pouring from his clothes, but he was still standing.

He glared at the Warden, who stood with his back turned, his eyes closed and his face tilted towards the sun, apparently uninterested. It must have taken all of Dain's resolve not to rush forward and push him to his death, but he had clearly learned some hard lessons in the days since he came to the Wall. There was a tense silence as everyone waited for the Warden's next command.

'The day is wasting,' he said.

And then he strode away, towards the gatehouse at the eastern end of the Wall, his sword flashing as it bounced at his hip.

The others began to disperse, hurried by guards who kept one hand permanently on their sword hilts. Dain stepped out of the cage, gave Ash and Bronwyn a quick nod, then headed towards the opposite end of the Wall, where a huge block of stone sat amongst a mess of ropes and harnesses.

Less than a minute later, only one man remained where the crowd had been. He had a bald head and heavily scarred cheeks. He stared at Ash as though he intended to say something.

But then he turned away. A moment later, he was lost amongst the bustle of bodies.

16

By the time the bell rang at midday Ash's shoulders burned, his arms ached, and his palms stung. For hours he had lugged pails of mortar from a vast trough to the place where the next block was to be laid. A vast barrel of water sat close to the trough, and each time he neared it his tongue seemed to roll in his mouth like a clump of sand. He had drunk his pitcher of water by mid-morning, and the thirst that came to plague him was the worst he had ever known. His skull seemed to shrink. A shrill sound pierced every thought. His insides griped. Apart from the small bowl of thin gruel that had been served shortly after sunrise, Ash had eaten nothing.

He dropped his pails beside the trough before the bell had stopped chiming. He gasped as sweat and air aggravated the open blisters on his fingers. Others hurried to the water tubs and dipped their pitchers. The guards stood nearby with swords drawn, watching closely.

A couple of small children made their way along the Wall carrying large baskets. Hands reached in, plucking out fist-sized clumps of something beige.

'Bread,' Bronwyn said, coming over to stand beside him. 'One of the others told me.'

Ash looked at her. She had been tasked with tramping the mortar to keep it from setting while the next block was brought up. Her lower legs were crusty and dusty. Flecks dotted her arms and face and clung to her hair.

'How was your morning?' Ash said.

Bronwyn looked down at herself. She held her hands out in despair and shrugged. 'Yours?'

'About the same. Although I can't shrug.'

They collected a piece of bread from one of the passing baskets, filled their pitchers at the water tub, and sat on the edge of the Wall with their legs dangling over the side. They looked out across the landscape, towards the Pikes, squinting into the sun. Far below their feet, the guards' settlement lay nestled at the base of the Wall, but neither Ash nor Bronwyn could look down without a queasy sensation swooping through their stomachs.

Ash tore off a chunk of bread with his teeth, chewed it, and washed it down with a gulp of water.

'Not bad,' he said. 'Bit dry.'

Bronwyn peered closely at her own piece. 'I wonder how it's made?'

Ash forgot that he couldn't shrug and ended up wincing in reply.

'Can you believe what Dain did earlier?' Bronwyn asked.

Ash shook his head, wondering at the Wall's power to inspire such a transformation. 'I thought we were going to have to pick someone.'

'So did I.' Bronwyn grinned. 'Although I probably would have picked Dain if I'd spotted him.'

Ash looked at the fading bruise around her eye and did his best to match her smile.

'I am sorry, you know,' Bronwyn said. 'About this.'

Again, Ash tried to smile. 'Me too.'

'Not just this,' Bronwyn said, grinding a knuckle into the Wall. 'I mean, I'm sorry that we didn't find what you thought we'd find. The Ancestors. The Four Fathers. The Kingdom. You might not believe me, but I was kind of hoping you would be right and I would be wrong. I wanted somewhere new to live just as much as you. Somewhere to belong. I was beginning to *believe*, after Samuel said it was real, and—'

'Don't,' Ash said. This time he managed a small smile. 'It's okay.'

Bronwyn nodded. They ate their bread in silence, resisting the urge to drink too much; the sun was high and hot, and it promised to be a gruelling afternoon.

As they ate, other people came to sit on the edge of the Wall. A boy that Ash recognised from Last Village came and sat beside him. His name was Robin, son of Quinn. Robin had never been one of Ash's tormentors – thanks, Ash suspected, to his father's influence – but he could hardly be counted as a friend either. So it was a surprise when he broke his bread in half and offered a piece to Ash.

'What's that for?' Ash said. His eyes flitted from the bread to the boy's face, which was freckly and framed by a tangle of ginger hair.

'For you.' He nodded towards Bronwyn. 'And your friend, if she's hungry.'

Ash peered past the boy, wary of a trap. There were others from Last Village on the far side of Robin, but none of them took any notice of the offering. They didn't seem interested in Ash at all.

'Go on,' Robin said. 'Take it.'

Ash took the bread. He turned it over in his hands. He sniffed it.

Robin laughed. 'It's not been poisoned, if that's

what you're worried about.'

As if to prove his point, he took a giant bite out of his own piece. That was good enough for Bronwyn, who took the bread from Ash and broke a chunk off for herself before handing the remainder back. Ash frowned.

'But . . . why?'

'First day on the Wall is tough, and you looked hungry when you got here.'

'But it's . . .' Ash trailed off. He couldn't think of a way to express himself that didn't feel like he was invoking a curse that had only just been lifted. 'But it's me.'

He cringed, but Robin simply shrugged.

'I think we've all got bigger problems now.'

He glanced at something behind Ash and Bronwyn. They turned just in time to see the Warden shove someone to the ground: a woman with unruly, short brown hair. Her pitcher spilled across the dusty stone in a dark circle.

'Move!' the Warden said, stepping over her as she scrambled out of his way. Ash and Bronwyn averted their eyes, keeping their backs to the Warden as he passed.

'Is he always like that?' Bronwyn asked, as soon as it was safe to do so.

Robin shook his head. 'No. He's normally worse. She got off lightly.'

Ash glanced back over his shoulder. The woman with short hair dusted herself off and stooped to collect her empty pitcher. She joined a huddle of people he didn't recognise, and he watched as each of them surreptitiously poured a splash of water from their own pitcher into hers.

He thought about this small act of kindness, and Dain's transformation, and the unexpected kinship he suddenly felt with the people of his village – with everyone on the Wall – and wondered why it had taken something so dire to bring about such change.

But then he caught sight of the man with scarred cheeks, his bald head gleaming, beads of sweat twinkling in his short, patchy beard, and realised that this newfound camaraderie didn't extend to everyone.

'Do you know anything about that man?' he asked Robin. 'The one with the scars?'

Robin covered his eyes and squinted. 'Not much. His name's Mason. Been here a long time, I think. Why?'

Ash watched as Mason downed his pitcher of water in a series of long gulps. He lowered his head suddenly, and Ash looked away. But he knew he had been caught staring. He *sensed* the man's eyes on him.

'No reason. I just didn't recognise him.'

Robin smiled ruefully. 'I'm sure it won't be long before you get acquainted.'

'What do you mean?'

'You heard the Warden: nobody leaves the Wall.' He looked down at the sheer drop beneath his feet. 'And the Wall is small.'

Ash gulped. He had an ugly, impulsive wish to see Mason sprawled out between the buildings far below. He still felt watched, but he resisted the temptation to check.

The bell clanged, making Ash and Bronwyn jump.

'You'll get used to that soon enough,' Robin said, standing up. He held out his hands and helped Ash and Bronwyn to their feet. 'Are you going to eat that or not?'

Ash looked down at the piece of bread in his hand. 'Thanks,' he said, and stuffed it in his mouth.

The pails were always heavy, whether they were empty or full. By late afternoon, Ash was in so much pain he could have wept: his body ached, his palms bled, his eyes stung. But he knew crying would do him no good. *To cry is a crime, to spit is a sin.* Instead, he focused on putting one foot in front of the other. He knew all too well what the punishment would be if he were to stop. The cage hung in the centre of the Wall, waiting.

The sun dipped below the western hills and still they went about their work. It wasn't until another hour had passed, and the sky was a dusty purple, that the Warden finally rang the bell.

Large, steaming cauldrons were brought up from below and Ash joined the nearest queue. When he reached the front a portion of stew was ladled into a bowl and passed to him. It was thin enough to drink. Small pieces of something unidentifiable floated on the surface, but Ash was too hungry to question what they might be. It was impossible, with the gnawing pain in his stomach, to imagine anything he wouldn't eat.

He gulped the stew down, being careful not to spill a drop, and then wiped his bowl with a chunk of bread. He placed the empty bowl in a tub of murky liquid beside the cauldron. His raw fingers stung as they touched the water. He joined another queue and refilled his pitcher.

Ash drank deeply – drank until his stomach felt bloated and awkward. He had promised himself that he would ration this pitcher, but now he found himself unable to stop – unable to think about the future, about how thirsty he would be a few hours or minutes from now.

Bronwyn came over just as he finished the last mouthful.

'You two,' a voice said.

Ash and Bronwyn turned to find Dain behind them. His shirt was dark with the sweat of his labours: two thick swathes crossed his chest, forming an X that marked where the harness had pressed against his torso.

'Come with me,' he said. 'I'll show you where you'll be sleeping.'

Ash and Bronwyn followed him past groups of people huddled together, sipping from pitchers and talking in quiet, dejected tones. Many simply sat on the stone floor, their backs arched, their heads hanging low.

Dain turned towards the reservoir and dropped nimbly over the edge of the Wall. A ladder led down to a suspended walkway of rough planks. Ash counted almost a dozen shacks clinging to the side of the Wall, but he knew there were more further along, concealed in shadow. The water below was black, and its gentle waves chuckled like little devils as they bumped against the stone.

'Come on,' Dain called. 'It's easier if you don't look down.'

Ash and Bronwyn exchanged a glance.

'Well, we can't sleep up here,' Bronwyn said.

Ash watched her descend, the ladder rocking under her weight. Ash hesitated, steeled himself, hesitated again. He did not trust himself to climb down in the dark, and the longer he dithered, the larger his doubt grew.

'You'll be all right,' Dain called. 'One rung at a time.'

Ash took a deep breath, grasped the top rung with a sore palm, and climbed down.

He forgot all about the pain in his hands and arms and shoulders the moment he found himself out over the water. In the darkness, the lake resembled a giant, bottomless pit. If he fell now, it would be a long time before he hit the water. But he did not fall. His feet touched the planks of the boardwalk, and all at once the aching and trembling in his muscles returned.

'Well done,' Dain said. 'Knew you had it in you. This way.'

They made their way along the boardwalk. Ash and Bronwyn trailed their fingertips along the vast stone blocks. There was no rope or rail to stop them from falling into the water, and Ash couldn't help but wonder how many people had come off the Wall after a long day and stumbled or tripped . . . and found themselves too weak to catch themselves – found themselves falling. A scream and a splash. He shook the thought away. Such an abundance of water was terrifying enough, but to imagine the ghosts that might lie beneath its black surface made Ash's skin prickle with fear.

They followed the walkway as it kinked around the shacks, taking care not to trip on the uneven planks. Dain stopped outside the third shack he came to and waited for Ash and Bronwyn to catch up. Inside, a lantern hung from the ceiling, throwing yellow light on to four bunk beds. One of them was occupied by two young men who might have been brothers, they looked so alike. Dain introduced them as Piper and Macauley. They both gave a grim nod. An elderly man slept in the bottom berth of the bunk diagonally opposite: 'Eric,' Dain informed them, just as someone jumped down from the bed above.

Ash recognised her as the woman who had been shoved to the ground by the Warden.

'Name's Jane,' she said, holding out her hand. 'Welcome to the Wall.'

Ash and Bronwyn introduced themselves, and Jane

gave each of them a firm handshake. Ash winced, and Jane quickly let go.

'Sorry about that,' she said, with a smirk. 'My palms are tough as leather now – you forget how gruelling the first few days can be.' She grasped his wrists and tilted his hands to the light. They looked as though he had spent the day scaling a jagged rockface. 'Nasty. Here, try this.' Jane reached up to the foot of her bunk and retrieved a small bowl of something pale and waxy.

'Is that—'

'Mutton fat,' Jane said, lifting out a scoop on her fingertips. 'I skim it off the broth and keep a little by for medicinal use. Cuts, sunburn, knotty shoulders . . .' She glanced up: the roguish smile was still on her face. 'But if you think you're getting a massage, you can think again.' She wiped the fat on to his right hand. 'There. Just rub it in slowly. It'll help you heal.'

Ash did so. The relief was almost instantaneous. 'Thank you.'

'We're all on the same side now. It's us against them.' She looked at the ceiling, but her meaning was clear: it's us against the guards. Us against the Warden.

Us. It was a strange new concept to Ash, but he liked it.

Jane pulled herself up on to her bunk, lay down, and cupped her hands behind her head.

'That's right,' Dain said. The shack was small, and it forced Ash and Bronwyn to stand awkwardly close to him. Neither of them knew what to say.

'Thanks for this morning,' Ash said, after a short pause. 'For helping us.'

Dain waved it away. 'It's like Jane says: it's us against them now. Besides, I meant what I said to the Warden. I owed you something after all those years of . . . Well, you know what I mean.'

Ash nodded. He did. But his own suffering suddenly seemed unimportant. They were all suffering now.

'What happened in Last Village?' he said. 'Everyone was just . . . gone.'

Dain shook his head. 'They used the cover of the storm – went from door to door, dragging people from their beds. They must have ambushed Quinn first – he was on watch at the Northern Post – so there weren't no alarm. Not that we would have heard it above the storm. There were only about ten of them in total, but they wore their swords and you don't need many men if they're armed right. Same thing must have happened in your village.' He looked to Bronwyn.

Bronwyn dropped her eyes to the floor and nodded.

'I thought you'd both got away when you weren't with us the next morning,' Dain said. 'How'd they get you?'

'We were betrayed by someone we met on our journey north,' Ash said.

'You were coming to find us?' The impressed – and slightly surprised – note in Dain's voice was hard to miss.

'Something like that,' Ash said. He cleared his throat and glanced around the shack. No one seemed to be paying much attention to their conversation, but he wished he could ask the next question without an audience. 'What happened to the Priestess?'

Dain's face fell. He rubbed a hand over his black beard. 'You saw her?'

Ash nodded. Dain drew in a deep breath.

'To tell the truth, I don't know for sure what happened. Maybe she refused to come, or maybe they wanted to make an example of her. All I know is they took her down to the pool and, well, you know the rest.' Dain shook his head. 'She's with the Four Fathers now.'

There was a long silence, broken only by the soft snores coming from Eric's bunk. The sound reminded

Ash and Bronwyn just how tired they were. They yawned simultaneously.

'It's been a long day,' Dain said. 'You two can sleep there.' He pointed to the bunk bed in the far corner. 'I wouldn't call it comfortable, but it's a place to rest, and no doubt better than wherever you've been sleeping on your way here.'

They stepped over to the bunk bed. If Ash and Bronwyn had been carrying any possessions, this would have been the time to find a home for them. But everything had been left behind in Samuel's cave.

'Which do you want?' Ash said.

Both bunks looked equally unappealing: five boards beneath a thin blanket of rough sacking.

'I don't really want either,' Bronwyn said. She scratched her head. A piece of dried mortar fell to the boards between her feet. She sighed. 'I'll take the bottom one.'

'Okay,' Ash said, even though the short ladder to the top bunk filled his aching body with dismay.

They were just about to turn in when someone stepped into the shack. What few noises there were stopped suddenly. Even Eric's snoring abated. It was as though a feral dog had snuck into a cosy home and curled up beside the hearth.

Ash and Bronwyn turned. In the doorway, his bald head brushing against the lintel, stood Mason. He looked at Ash with unsmiling eyes. Then, to Ash's horror, he lowered himself on to the bunk by the door. He lay down, interlocked his hands on his stomach, and closed his eyes.

Dain peered over the edge of the bunk above and glanced at Ash. He pointed at his eyes with two fingers, then pointed at Mason. His meaning was clear: *Watch out for him*. It was a warning that Ash did not need.

17

Ash woke with a start.

He had forgotten where he was, and it took a few seconds to regain his bearings. Then the crushing reality hit home. He was on the Wall. He could not see Bronwyn from his bunk, and he suddenly felt very alone. He had never felt so alone. He was without his parents, without Helena: a true orphan of the world. His despair was so absolute that he very nearly prayed to the Four Fathers. But the Four Fathers either did not exist, or did not care that he existed. There was no use in praying to them. They had forsaken him. Forsaken them all.

A bell clanged high above, and he heard the others stir. For several seconds he did not move; he stared at the ceiling, waiting for some kind of reprieve. It did not come. He felt a hand on his arm, and slowly rolled his head to see Bronwyn's upturned face.

'It's time to get up,' she said, softly.

Ash returned his gaze to the boards above his head. 'What's the point?'

It wasn't Bronwyn who replied: it was Dain.

'The point is that if you don't, you'll find yourself in the cage. And maybe some of us will be sent down too, for letting you stay in bed when we could have roused you. Now, come on, lad. You're a Last Villager, and we're made of sterner stuff than that.'

Ash looked towards Dain but his eye was caught by Mason, who sat on the edge of his bunk, pulling his boots on. He looked at Ash steadily. That look, and the thought of getting someone else ducked in the cage, prompted Ash to sit up and swing his legs over the side of the bed.

He dropped down from the top bunk – and his knees nearly buckled beneath him. His whole body ached, his shoulders were in agony, and his hands felt as though he had snatched a burning log directly from the fire. The prospect of carrying pails of mortar all day was one that he could not face, and yet he had no choice but to climb the ladder and face it.

'That's the spirit,' Dain said, giving Ash's shoulder a squeeze. Ash winced. 'You'll be all right. I'll watch out for you.'

The others filed out of the shack. Dain cast a glance over his shoulder before leaning in close.

'Listen. I haven't been here long, but I've been here long enough to know that the Warden has his spies.' He cast a meaningful glance at Mason's bunk. 'I suspect the Warden likes to know what's said in these shacks, and I'm sure it wouldn't take much – a bit of fear, a bit of food – to get some answers. So just be careful what you say around people you don't know, understand?'

Ash and Bronwyn exchanged a glance, then nodded.

'Good.' Dain checked over his shoulder once more. Outside, the sound of footsteps on the boardwalk began to fade. 'The other thing I need you to understand is that we're going to get off this wall.'

Ash didn't know how to respond. All that came out of his open mouth was a strangled noise of surprise.

'I've already started finding others, but it's slow work. We've got to be careful: if the Warden catches wind of an uprising he'll crush us.' He glanced once more at Mason's bunk. 'We've got the numbers. All we need is to bring the different villages together to fight for the same cause: freedom. That's what I'm trying to do.'

Ash's heart pounded: he felt exhilarated and exhausted.

'What do you need us to do?' Bronwyn asked.

Dain smiled. 'For now, nothing. I know it's tough up there, but I need you to keep your heads down and keep going. Do the work and don't complain. The Warden needs to believe he's broken our spirit.' He looked from Bronwyn to Ash. 'But I need you to be ready, when the time comes.'

'We will be,' Ash said.

'I know.' Dain straightened up and placed his hands on his hips. 'Right, come on. No point arousing suspicion by being late.'

They followed Dain up to the Wall, where their work – and the Warden – were waiting for them.

The first shuttle was the hardest, and the rest were not much easier. The pails tortured Ash's palms and stretched his aching shoulders. Within the hour, his shirt was soaked with sweat. Salt got into his eyes and the raw blisters of his fingers, and the sting made his breath come in hissing gasps.

Breakfast was brought up, and Ash hated his stomach for squirming in pleasure at the prospect of such a meagre meal. He drank the gruel and sipped at his pitcher of water, determined to make it last till midday.

But when lunchtime arrived, and he sat down on the

edge of the Wall, his pitcher had been empty for a long time. He was too tired to talk to Bronwyn or Robin or any of the others who sat nearby. They ate their bread in silence. All his rebellious spirit from the morning was gone, drained from him like the sweat from his pores. He wondered how ready he could possibly be when the time came, if he was always going to feel this exhausted.

The afternoon was long and hot and painfully bright. He longed to stop, to rest, to sleep. He came close to dropping his pails late in the afternoon, but he glanced up just as the Warden passed by on one of his patrols. The sight sent a spurt of adrenaline through his veins, giving him the strength to go on.

When the end of the day finally came and the bell was rung once more, Ash devoured his stew in silence, drank his pitcher of water, and collapsed into bed.

The next day was the same, as was the one that followed. And the one after that.

The blisters on his hands bled. The muscles in his arms and shoulders grew tender, then firm. The world shrank to a narrow strip of stone. Mason watched him from afar. To be looked at – *observed* – with such silent curiosity when his days were so dull, and so plainly not his own, was infuriating. Ash was careful never to be caught alone with him: in the shack or on the Wall.

The days began to bleed into one another. They were all the same. There were duckings almost daily. It seemed to be the Warden's favourite pastime. He took great pleasure in listening to the hiss of the rope as it unspooled its length, the splash as the cage hit the water, the ensuing silence. Sometimes, he ordered someone to haul the cage up, then ducked that person for neglecting their duties. The guards could pass an entire afternoon in this way. An entire month of afternoons.

Ash lay in his bunk, looking at the ceiling. Dain paced the shack. Every night, he went out to recruit for his uprising, whispering and plotting and cajoling. But tonight he was trapped; a storm raged outside, preventing him from visiting the others.

'It's taking too long,' he muttered.

Nobody said anything, but everyone was listening – including Mason. Dain strode back and forth in the guttering light of the lantern.

'Will you sit down?' Eric said. 'Some of us are trying to sleep.'

'Sleep? What for? So you can work all the harder for your *masters* tomorrow?'

'They're your masters too.'

Dain reached the door and spat into the storm. 'They're not my masters. I've never had a master and I'm not starting now.'

'Why don't you go and tell the Warden, then?' Eric said. 'I'm sure he'll listen harder than anyone here.'

'Don't be a fool.'

'You're the fool,' Eric said, his voice shaky with despair. 'How long do you think our disobedience would go unpunished? You're endangering us all. The Kings—'

'I do not care about the so-called Kings!' Dain brought his fist down on the wall of the shack and the whole thing shook. He breathed heavily, his nostrils flaring, and looked from face to face. 'Who says they even exist? What if they're just a story invented by the Warden to keep us afraid?'

Nobody responded.

Dain shook his head. 'I can't stay here. There's work to be done.' And with that he clutched his tunic about his throat and stomped out of the shack, into the storm.

For several minutes, the others lay in their bunks,

listening to the wind howl and the wood creak. The lantern burned down to almost nothing. There was something almost cosy about the shack at times like these: its soft light and shelter, its quiet, familiar sounds. Fatigue swaddled each occupant like a thick blanket.

Ash was on the cusp of unconsciousness when the voice spoke: deep and unfamiliar. It woke him as fully as if he'd fallen from his bunk. He sat up and looked across the room.

Mason lay on his bunk, his hands crossed on his chest. Had everyone else not turned their attention to him, Ash would have been tempted to believe he'd imagined the voice.

'What did you say?' Jane said.

Mason took a deep breath before hauling himself up to sit on the edge of his bunk. 'The Kings,' he said, addressing the large hands that hung between his knees. 'They do exist.'

'And what makes you so sure?' Bronwyn asked.

Mason looked up. The dying light caught his scars and threw long shadows across his cheeks. 'Because I was one.'

The others exchanged glances, unsure of what to say. Ash stared at Mason. He was wary of believing anything this man told them, and yet he found himself desperate to know more.

'You used to live in the Kingdom?' Bronwyn asked.

Mason nodded. There was another pause: clearly, everyone else was deciding whether to believe him or not too.

'What's it like?' Jane asked.

Mason closed his eyes. A faint smile played at the corner of his mouth. 'It's like going back in time – to the way things were. They grow things: plants and crops. Flowers, even – just for their beauty. There are animals too. Not many, but enough to make your heart glad. No birds, sadly. At least, none that can fly. They kept trying to escape.' He opened his eyes. His smile was small and confused and full of pain. 'As a child, I used to find them around the edge of the dome all . . . broken.'

'If it was so idyllic,' Macauley said, rubbing the thick muscle of his shoulder, 'why did you leave?'

'I didn't leave,' Mason said. 'I was exiled.'

'Why?' Bronwyn said.

'I objected to things the others were doing.'

'What things?'

Mason stretched out his arms. 'This. I remember when the Wall was nothing more than an idea. A group of us tried to stop them: we knew there were other people who depended on the river to survive. But they wouldn't listen. They went ahead with the dam despite our protestations. Being sent here was our punishment.'

'Who are the others?' Piper asked. There was an edge to his voice: he either didn't believe Mason, or believed him and didn't trust him as a consequence. 'I've never heard anyone else claim to be a King.'

'It was a long time ago.' Mason let his arms fall. 'They're not here any more.'

'Not here?'

Mason hung his head. 'No. I'm the last of us.'

Ash's curiosity outweighed his caution. 'What are the Kings like?' he said. 'The ones who live there now?'

Mason looked at him, and it made Ash realise that he had, till now, been avoiding his gaze. 'They're selfish and cruel.'

'You would say that,' Jane said. 'They sent you here.'

Mason smiled wearily. 'I suppose I would, but it's true. They are people who can't see beyond their own privilege. The Kingdom was created by selfish people for selfish reasons.'

'What do you mean?' Bronwyn asked.

'Many years ago, when it became apparent just what

227

kind of world our ancestors had created, a group of very powerful people decided to build a haven to protect themselves from the worst of what was to come. They could have helped a great many people with their wealth, but they thought only of themselves. Their descendants are no different.'

'Except for you?' Ash said.

The flame in the lantern hissed and died. The shack was thrown into almost total darkness.

'Except for me.'

18

'What do you think?' Ash said.

Bronwyn dangled her legs over the edge of the Wall and chewed a mouthful of bread. She looked to where Mason stood, drenched in sweat, partly obscured by the shimmering haze. The day was hot. Even the guards – with their wide-brimmed hats and idleness – wore dark patches of sweat around their necks. They drank from the tubs incessantly, but it did nothing to cool their tempers.

'I'm not sure. I suppose he could be telling the truth.'

'But you don't believe him?'

Bronwyn shrugged. 'I just think it's odd he waited until Dain left before saying anything. If he *was* exiled from the Kingdom, you'd have thought he'd want to be involved in Dain's plans.'

Ash nodded. 'You're right.' He glanced at Mason. 'It doesn't make sense.'

They both drank a gulp of water. Robin came and sat beside Bronwyn. He looked tired – or more tired than was usual.

'Long night?' Ash said.

Robin yawned before responding. 'There's a gap between a couple of the planks right above my bunk, and when there's a storm the wind makes this annoying whistling sound. I didn't fall asleep until early this morning.' He tore off a chunk of bread with his teeth. 'It didn't help that Dain came by again, trying to start a riot.'

Ash and Bronwyn laughed.

'I mean, who goes out *in a storm* to do that?'

'I suppose you can't question his commitment,' Ash said.

Robin took a swig of water. 'I suppose not. My father thinks he's trying to make up for what happened in the village.'

Ash frowned. 'What do you mean?'

Robin swallowed another mouthful before responding. 'I think he wants to be the one to rescue us because he feels responsible for us being here.'

'Why? Because he was an Elder of Last Village?'

Robin shook his head. 'No. Because it happened on his watch.'

Ash and Bronwyn exchanged a glance. 'Wasn't it your father who was on watch?'

Robin scowled. 'No. Of course not. It was Dain.'

'Are you sure?' Bronwyn said.

'It was a pretty memorable night. I know what happened.'

Maybe Quinn lied to his son? Ash thought. *Or maybe Dain was too ashamed to admit that it was him?* He looked around, trying to find Quinn, but instead saw something that made his heart stutter in his chest.

'Oh no,' he said.

Bronwyn and Robin turned. It was Eric. Two guards were dragging him towards the cage. He kicked wildly and clawed at the hands that held him, but they were too strong. There was no chance of breaking free. As they neared the cage Eric began to curse loudly. More people turned to watch. The two guards slung him in the cage.

That was when Eric gave up cursing and began to beg.

'Please,' he said. 'Please.'

The door clanged shut. The bolt slid home. The arm swung out over the water.

'Please,' Eric said.

The lever dropped.

And so did the cage.

A whirr of rope. A distant splash. Then silence.

The Warden arrived. He took his hat from his head and lazily fanned himself.

'Who is it?' he asked.

The guards shrugged. 'One of the old ones.'

The Warden nodded. He glanced around and saw that all eyes were on him. He returned his hat to his head and tweaked its position.

Then he stepped to the bell and rang it.

'Back to work,' he announced. 'The day is wasting.'

Then he stalked away, his heels *tock-tock-tock*ing against the stone blocks of the Wall.

Dain paced the shack, indignant: a one-man hurricane.

'Do you see now what will become of us?' he said, pointing to Eric's empty bunk. 'Which of us is next, do you suppose? Is it you, Piper? Or you, Macauley? You hide your injury well, up on the Wall, but how long will it be before it begins to get the better of you? How long before the Warden notices you're not hauling quite as much as before? And how long after that will he be looking to replace you, like a broken roof tile?'

The men fidgeted and struggled to meet Dain's wide-eyed stare.

'Or maybe it will be one of the young 'uns?' Dain said, gesturing towards Ash and Bronwyn. 'How long before the Warden realises they get their full measure of gruel and bread and stew, but give only half the work of a full-grown man?'

'Stop it,' Jane said. Her eyebrows were bunched tight. 'You'll scare them.'

'They ought to be scared,' Dain said. 'If we don't act soon, none of us will make it off this infernal wall.'

'So what do you suggest?' Mason said. He sat up, squeezing the edge of his bunk in two great fists.

Dain emitted a short, bitter laugh. 'You think I'd tell someone like you?'

Mason tilted his head to the side. 'What do you mean by that?'

Dain scoffed. 'Oh, I think you know. The Warden has his pets. And who's got a better reason to whisper in the Warden's ear than you – a former King?' He must have noticed a flash of confusion or fear cross Mason's face, because he smiled suddenly. 'Do you think they'll take you back one day, if you make sure the Wall gets built? If you prove your loyalty?'

'You are mistaken.' Mason's voice was calm.

'Am I? So you intend to join me? You plan to rise up against them?'

Mason took a deep breath. Eventually, he shook his head. 'I have been here a great deal longer than you, Dain. Many people have tried to escape. Some of them even made it off the Wall. But they were all brought back, one way or another. Where is there to go, after all? And when they catch you, they'll make an example of you.' He looked at Eric's empty bunk. 'You must know that already.'

'So you'd rather work till you die?'

Mason drew in a long, slow breath that caused his chest to swell. He exhaled through his nostrils. He kept his eyes trained on the rough wooden floor.

'What I would rather doesn't matter. I've been on the Wall too long – seen too many good people die because of it – to think I've got a say.'

When he looked up, his eyes were fixed on Ash. The look was so tired – so earnest – that it caused the frown to fall from Ash's face.

'Is that why you're trying to discourage the rest of us?' Dain asked. 'Because you can't bear for anyone else to do what you won't? What you can't?'

Mason lay back on his bunk and cupped his hands behind his head. 'Do what you will, Dain. Believe what you want. Make your plans, but keep me out of them.'

Dain's face was fixed in a look of contempt. 'Your lies may fool some people, but not me. I'd sleep with one eye open, if I were you.'

Mason said nothing, only closed his eyes. Both of them.

19

Ash awoke in the night to a miraculous sound. At first, he couldn't place it, and the moment he did he was sure he must be dreaming. He sat up and looked to the open doorway.

Little drops of silver fell from the lintel. He listened to a gentle patter on the roof, listened as the patter grew to a roar.

He jumped down from his bunk and ran out on to the boardwalk. The rain soaked him in seconds. He turned his face to the sky, mouth open, and let the droplets fall on his tongue and splash against his eyelids. There was no wind. It was the rarest of things: a downpour. A gift from the sky. He opened his eyes and watched the surface of the lake jitter and jump in the moonlight. He breathed in its freshness, drank in its promise.

He did not notice Mason behind him. Not, at least, until he spoke.

'I have been waiting a long time for an opportunity like this.'

Ash spun around, his long hair whipping across his face like a cat o' nine tails. He saw the dark, hulking shape of Mason, burnished by the moon's brilliance. Remembered the wariness that weariness had allowed him to forget. This was the man who had observed him since his very first day on the Wall. He took half a step backwards, felt the edge of the boardwalk, the long drop to the water below. His balance began to tip.

Mason stretched out a hand and caught him firmly by the arm. 'Careful,' he said.

'What do you want?'

'To talk.'

Ash glanced fearfully over his shoulder. 'I'm not the spy, if that's what this is about.'

'I know,' Mason said. He was still holding Ash's arm, but his grip was no longer quite so fierce. He looked into Ash's face the same way he had all those weeks ago: it was a look that made Ash feel small and scrutinised.

'You're his son, aren't you?'

Ash felt his flesh prickle. He opened his mouth but nothing came out.

Mason smiled. 'You look just like him.'

'You knew my father?'

Mason nodded. 'He was a good man.'

'You . . .' Ash didn't know what to say. Something Helena said on her last night echoed in his mind: *You are good, Ash.* He felt dizzy. He was suddenly glad of the hand that held him. But then hope turned to disappointment. 'It's not possible. My father disappeared a long time ago.'

'It is possible,' Mason said. 'He was here, on the Wall.'

Ash tried to peer deep into Mason's eyes, to see whether this was the truth or some cruel trick, but the rain made his eyelids twitch and his vision blur. But it didn't really matter: Mason had said the fatal word.

'Was?'

Mason nodded.

'What happened to him?'

Mason looked around to check they were still alone. Further along, a child stood outside one of the shacks, their hands cupped before them to catch the rain.

'Come on,' Mason said, turning away. He walked along the outside edge of the boards, leaving a space for Ash on the inside, beside the Wall. Ash hesitated before following, but only for a moment.

'Your father wasn't like most of the people who are

brought to the Wall. Most of them arrive here fearful and dejected. It's no surprise – many of them have lost everything: their homes, their gods, their freedom. But your father was different.' Mason let out a deep, melodious laugh. 'It took four of them to bring him in, and they looked extremely relieved to be rid of him. I don't think the ordeal was worth whatever price the Warden paid.'

The image made Ash smile, but then he remembered that he did not know how the story ended.

'Your father didn't shrink the way other people do. Most people, you can see the fight trickling out of them with each bead of sweat. But your father never seemed to tire. He worked as though the work was light.' Mason fell silent as they passed another shack. 'But all the while he had his mind on something else: escape. He was planning to return to his village. To you.'

Ash shook his head. 'I don't think so. My father deserted our village.'

Mason raised his eyebrows. 'Someone who is dragged off by four men can hardly be accused of desertion.'

'They must have picked him up further north. He abandoned his post. Ask anyone from Last Village.'

'Someone like Dain?' Ash opened his mouth to

answer, but Mason wasn't finished. 'Do you really believe your father would abandon you?'

Ash couldn't meet Mason's gaze. He looked out at the expanse of water instead.

'What happened next? You said my father wanted to escape. Did he try?'

'He did.'

'But they caught him.'

Mason ran a hand over his bald head.

'In the end. The Warden took his escape personally: he led the search party himself.'

Ash swallowed. 'Did he . . . ?' His courage failed him. For so long he'd been sure that not knowing was the worst part, but now he was on the brink of understanding he wanted nothing more than to retreat into ignorance.

They came to the end of the boardwalk. Behind them, all along its length, people were stepping out into the downpour.

Mason rested a hand on Ash's shoulder. 'Your father once told me he'd sooner die in the wild than here on the Wall. I'm afraid to say I think he got his wish. He never came back.'

Ash was glad that his long hair hid his face. 'Why

should I believe you?' he asked.

Mason shrugged. 'Why would I lie?'

Ash gave a glum nod. He lowered himself down and sat on the edge of the boardwalk.

Mason sat down beside him. 'I'm sorry to be the one to tell you.'

'Why didn't you tell me sooner?'

'I've been trying to catch you on your own for weeks. I didn't want to do it in the shack. It's not the kind of thing you want to hear with an audience.'

Rainwater dripped from the tips of Ash's hair, plummeting towards the dark water below.

'At first, I didn't know for sure that it was you, but any doubts I had didn't last long. The resemblance is uncanny: the expressions, the mannerisms – you even move in the same way.'

Ash nodded. The flashes of recognition that sometimes passed across the Warden's face suddenly made sense. The Warden had known his father – had killed his father.

Ash took a deep breath. Mason's words had wounded him, but there was comfort in them too. His father had been good. His father had managed to escape the Wall.

And he was like his father.

Ash lifted his head and turned to Mason. 'All this time I thought you had it in for me. You could try smiling once in a while.'

Mason laughed at that. 'Smiling doesn't come naturally when you've been on the Wall as long as I have, but I'll do my best.'

Behind them now, the length of the boardwalk was abuzz with people savouring the downpour. Nobody paid the two figures sitting at the end any attention.

'How long have you been here?' Ash said.

Mason scratched his waterlogged beard. 'Hard to say. I think it must be seven years since I was banished from the Kingdom. I was one of the first to be put to work. Started in the quarries, breaking rocks. Then hauling. Then tunnelling.'

'Is there really a pipe that takes water to the Kingdom?'

'There is. We had to blast our way beneath the hills. Dangerous work. Lost a lot of men.' Mason noticed the puzzled expression on Ash's face. 'You're wondering how you blast through something like a hill?'

Ash nodded.

'Explosives.'

The puzzled expression remained.

'They're made from a special powder that goes bang when it gets hot. They come in sticks or bricks. You light the fuse and run away.' He touched the smooth welts on his face. 'This is what happens when you don't run away fast enough – if you're lucky.'

Ash thought back to the mines, suddenly realising how those endless tunnels had been created. He gazed at the top of the Wall, high above. He tried to imagine the valley without it and couldn't. Those days were for ever in the past now. The Wall would stand long after the hands that built it had turned to dust.

'If only we had some explosives now,' he said.

Mason nodded. 'Indeed. I sometimes wonder how things might be different if I'd hidden some away while I was working on the tun—'

'Wait!' Ash sat up so quickly he nearly overbalanced and tumbled over the edge. Mason laid a hand on his shoulder. 'What? What is it?'

'You said that explosives come in bricks?'

'Yes. Or sticks.'

'And they're used for blasting holes in rock – to make tunnels?'

'Yes.'

'What do they look like?'

'It varies.' Mason narrowed his eyes. 'Why?'

Ash looked up, towards the hill at the eastern end of the Wall. He recalled the night he spent in Samuel's cave – remembered Samuel nibbling at the edge of a pale brick. A pale brick he had found in the mines.

'I think I know where to find some.'

Mason glanced over his shoulder. The commotion caused by the rain was loud and distant, but when he spoke he did so in a whisper. 'Where?'

Ash pointed. 'Up there.' He quickly explained his journey through the mines, and how he had come to be betrayed by Samuel. As he spoke, Mason's eyes grew wide.

'You carried a brick of explosives *and* a flaming torch?' He shook his head. 'I'm amazed you didn't blow yourself to smithereens.'

Ash stared at the high hump of rock, black against the overcast sky. A very simple idea was taking shape in his head. 'If we could somehow get that brick and bring it back here, we could destroy the Wall.'

'I'm afraid it's not that simple.'

'We've got to try!'

'I agree, but you need to understand how impossible what you're suggesting would be. Firstly, you don't know if it's still there: the brick might be gone. Even if it is still there, you'd have to get off the Wall undetected – which wouldn't be easy – and then back on to the Wall – which would probably be harder.'

'My father made it off the Wall.'

'He did. But he was also caught and killed by the Warden.'

Ash folded his arms across his chest. 'Go on.'

'Even if you somehow made it off the Wall, retrieved the brick, and made it back on to the Wall you'd still have to detonate the explosives.'

'Detonate?'

Mason nodded. 'Explosives normally have a fuse – some kind of cord or trail that allows you to ignite the charge without blowing yourself up too. You have to expose the explosives to heat to activate them.'

'So we'd need fire?'

'Something like that. It only takes a spark.'

Ash thought for a moment. The rain was beginning to ease. Soon they would have to return to the shack or risk arousing suspicion.

'What about the lantern in the shack?'

'Not exactly ideal, but let's say you could somehow use that flame to ignite the explosives: where are you going to plant the brick? You've only got one brick, right?'

'Yes.' Ash bit his lip. 'Where would be the best place?'

'Probably at the base of the Wall. Impossible on this side, but potentially possible on the dry side. You'd have to do it without anyone in the guards' settlement seeing you, of course. And the chances are that one brick wouldn't generate enough force to compromise the Wall. And remember, you've somehow got to transport a naked flame down a three-hundred-foot precipice too. That rules out doing it in the dark – you'd be like a beacon – so you'd have to do it in broad daylight.'

A familiar feeling of powerlessness began to sour Ash's enthusiasm, but the thought of giving up was unconscionable. The solution was so near. There had to be a way.

'What if I could do all those things? I know you said one brick might not be enough, but if it's our only chance then we've got to try it.'

Mason smiled. The steady procession of droplets falling from his beard began to slow with the lessening rain. Their time together was almost up.

'Let's say your plan works, and the brick blasts a hole in the bottom of the Wall. What happens to the dozens of people *on* the Wall – toiling beneath the sun, or asleep in their shacks?'

Ash let out a breath, and all the fight and hope and optimism fled from him.

'Unless you could somehow evacuate the Wall in advance without any of the guards noticing, they'd all be swept away or crushed. *We*'d all be swept away or crushed, Ash. And what would that achieve?'

Something dark swooped out of the sky before them – a manic shadow that was gone in an instant: a flap of wings, a blink of midnight. It disappeared so quickly that Ash began to doubt whether it had been anything more than a trick of the light. And yet his pounding heart insisted that it had been real, and the heart is harder to fool than the eyes.

Mason turned to look at Ash. They were both soaked to the skin, but it was too warm to shiver. 'Don't give up,' he said.

'It just felt like we were so close to ending all this.'

Mason stood up and patted a huge block of stone. 'Well, maybe we are. We built the Wall, I'm sure we can tear it down.'

Mason extended his hand. After a moment, Ash allowed himself to be hauled to his feet. It felt good to stand: he no longer felt quite so small. Ahead of him, all along the boardwalk, people were returning to their shacks.

'You go first,' Mason said. 'I'll be there in a few minutes.'

Ash took a step, but a strong hand stopped him from taking another. He turned back.

'And remember,' Mason said, 'it only takes a spark.'

20

Ash told Bronwyn about his conversation with Mason the following day, as they sat with their legs dangling over the edge of the Wall. Her initial shock turned to excitement as she learned about the explosives, but it was soon extinguished as Ash relayed just how impossible any attempt to destroy the Wall would be. By the end of his account, she felt as despondent as he did.

'I'm sorry about your father,' she said.

Ash gazed at the blocks between him and the ground, three hundred feet below, wondering which ones his father had laid. 'Thanks. I think I knew all along I'd never find him. It's kind of a relief, knowing that I won't. At least now I can let go.'

Ash heard himself say the words, but he had no idea whether he believed them or not. He had carried the idea of his father so far, and for so long, it was hard to imagine parting with the hope of seeing him again.

'How did he end up here?' Bronwyn asked. 'If Mason is telling the truth, and your father didn't abandon the village, what did happen?'

Ash shook his head; he had spent most of the night wondering the same thing. 'There's something we don't know,' he said. 'Something we're missing. The whole thing never made sense to me. My father was popular and respected before he disappeared – a hero. He had no reason to leave. So why did he?'

Bronwyn squinted into the sun. 'Maybe he didn't.'

Ash took his eyes from the long drop between his feet and glanced at Bronwyn, but she kept her eyes on the monstrous shape of the Pikes.

'What if the men who brought your father here abducted him from Last Village, like Mason said, and not from further north? He was on watch that night, right?'

Ash nodded.

'And he would have been all alone at the Northern Post?'

Again, Ash nodded.

'Maybe the kidnappers intended to take more people from the village, but your father somehow stopped them?'

'Mason did say that he fought them all the way. But if

that is what happened, why was everyone so quick to believe he deserted us? Why didn't anyone suggest he might have been taken?'

'Maybe they didn't know about the others . . . out there.'

'Helena knew. You heard what Vivienne said: she came from outside the village.'

'And from what you've told me, Helena had her doubts.'

'So why did she let people think my father was a coward and a traitor?'

Bronwyn brushed the crumbs from her tunic. She took a sip of water and cleared her throat. She took another sip.

'What?' Ash said.

Bronwyn took a deep breath. 'Can you imagine how frightened the villagers would have been if they'd thought kidnappers might come in the night to take them away? Maybe Helena let the rumours about your father spread because . . . well, because hate is easier than fear.'

Ash shook his head. There was a bitter taste in his mouth – a taste like blood. He wanted to spit but his mouth was as dry as the stone on which he sat. 'If that's true, then Helena is the reason why everyone hated me. Why children pelted me with stones and goaded me.'

'She's also the reason you weren't exiled: the person who gave you a home away from all the others.'

Tears pricked behind Ash's eyes, but he was determined not to cry. *To cry is a crime, to spit is a sin.*

'Why?' He forced the word out through gritted teeth. 'Why would she do that to me?'

Bronwyn shrugged. 'Maybe she thought you were strong enough to bear it. Maybe she thought you could serve the village in a way that most people couldn't.'

Ash bit his lip, and this time the blood he could taste was real. 'If she'd told the truth, we might have been ready the night they came for us all.'

Bronwyn nodded. 'Maybe. Or maybe it would have happened anyway, and the village would have spent all those years living in fear.'

'Helena knew nothing. She was wrong – wrong about the Four Fathers and the Kingdom. Wrong to let my father become a villain. Wrong to hide the truth from the village. Wrong to use me as a scapegoat.'

'I think so too,' Bronwyn said. 'But she wasn't wrong about everything.'

Ash's heart thudded in his chest. He let out a

sound that was part laugh, part snarl. 'So what did she get right?'

Bronwyn ignored the venom in Ash's question. Her voice was calm and quiet when she spoke. 'She was right about you.'

Ash sat in silence, his bitterness ebbing away.

'By taking the blame for what your father supposedly did, you saved your village from something terrible: years of uncertainty and fear.' Bronwyn paused. 'Maybe you can save them again.'

The bell rang behind them, and Bronwyn climbed to her feet. 'Come on,' she said, reaching out a hand. 'Up.'

Ash took a deep breath. Unbidden, his mind filled with something Helena had said on that final night.

As long as you breathe, it goes on. You have power as long as you are alive.

Ash took another deep breath. He climbed to his feet. He felt weak.

And yet you stand.

They, too, were Helena's words, and they gave him strength.

For weeks, Ash thought of that pale brick in the dark cave. That little package of potential. He fantasised about rubble – about a great surge of water being unleashed. And all the while he lugged pails of mortar, watching as yet another huge stone was added to the Wall.

Sometimes, he thought of his father. He thought of him every time he saw the Warden strut along the Wall, cruel and cocksure. And soon enough his thoughts turned to murder: his father's in the past, the Warden's in the future. It would be so easy – so satisfying – to push him . . . But the Wall would remain standing, even if the Warden fell. How many of the other guards were simply waiting for their turn in charge? There would be a new warden before the old one hit the ground. He would achieve nothing but a momentary satisfaction before that, too, was eliminated.

More than anything, he thought of Last Village: the pool glimmering on the valley floor; the squat buildings with their slate roofs; the church with its tumbledown graveyard; the sheep bleating on the slopes; the House on the Hill watching over it all like an attentive parent. He preferred to think of things the way they had been. He knew, of course, that the pool would be a dusty crater by now, and the buildings would be dilapidated, and the church no longer had a spire. The House on the Hill oversaw nothing but the village's decay. The sheep . . .

He wasn't sure about the sheep. On some days, he imagined them doing what they had always done: grazing, bleating, huddling together. They would be in such desperate need of a shear that even Tristan wouldn't be able to tell them apart. On other days, he envisaged what had probably happened. A pack of feral dogs, or perhaps just one, had crept into the village, and now there were no more sheep in Last Village, just as there were no more people.

But he preferred to think of things the way they had been.

He shuffled along the Wall, lost in memory. He was remembering how it felt to be immersed in the pool, to escape the sun's wrath, to be clean; remembering the way the ripples spread outwards from Helena's body as she lowered herself backwards, preparing to stream-dream; remembering the way the children jumped back so as not to let the water wash over their toes. These moments were so vivid that he began to wonder why he couldn't hear bleating, or the chuckle of the stream as it entered the pool, when he was roused by the distant rumble of thunder.

He looked about. It was late in the day. The air was thick and humid and promised violence. A wide bank of cloud crept up from the south, snagging the jagged tips of the Pikes and borrowing their blackness. Strong, unpredictable gusts began to buffet those on the Wall as they scurried about. The Warden stood on the very edge, watching the approaching storm. His face cracked into a smile: he seemed to enjoy teetering on the cusp of chaos. The steel-grey clouds folded and crowded over one another as they raced across the sky, like waves crashing towards a shore. A distant flash of lightning was followed several seconds later by an almighty boom.

'Tie everything down!' the Warden shouted. 'Make everything secure!'

They raced about, tethering ropes, securing carts, stowing tools. The sky darkened with nightmarish speed. There was another pulse of lightning – followed closely by thunder – and this time it was like a huge fist pounding against a door. The air pressure dropped suddenly, making Ash's scalp crawl and prickle.

'That's enough!' the Warden shouted. 'Back to your quarters!' He stepped away from the precipice and strode towards the gatehouse at the eastern end of the Wall. He glared at Ash as he passed. 'Now!'

Ash was slow to move, but his brain was whirring. Memories and thoughts and possibilities were colliding behind his eyes, as though kicked up and carried by the coming storm in an accelerating, ever-tightening vortex: Helena falling back into the pool, the lightning, an outward spread of ripples, the Burned Forest, the brick of explosives, the ruined church. And the same words, weaving through each thought and binding them together: *It only takes a spark*.

Bronwyn appeared beside him, her hair whipping about her head. 'Come on!'

All around them, people scurried to the ladders and dropped over the edge. Dain stood nearby, urging them to hurry.

'I know how to do it!' Ash shouted.

'What?'

'The Wall! I know how to bring it down!'

Bronwyn's eyes grew wide. Another fork of lightning splintered across the sky. 'How?'

'There's no time to explain! I need you to go to all the shacks! Tell everyone to be ready to leave!'

'When?'

'Tonight! Get Mason and Jane and Robin – anyone you trust – to help you!'

'How will I know when it's time?'

Ash glanced at the approaching storm, bearing down

on the Wall with frightening speed, then to the north, where the Kingdom lay concealed behind dark hills. 'If my plan works, you'll know.'

The Wall was almost deserted. The bell began to clang listlessly as the winds rose. It gave Ash an idea.

'I'll ring the bell, too, so there's a clear signal for everyone to evacuate.'

Bronwyn nodded.

'You two!' Dain called from the top of a nearby ladder. 'Get to the shack!'

They flinched as another almighty boom filled the air. A vicious gust shoved them so hard they staggered.

'I hope you know what you're doing,' Bronwyn said.

Ash couldn't answer truthfully, so he didn't answer at all. Another gust hit them, just as Dain shouted, 'Now!'

It was all the encouragement they needed. They rushed to the nearest ladder and Bronwyn dropped over the edge, quickly followed by Ash. The surface of the lake ruffled and shivered like the coat of some immense, glossy predator. Waves crashed into the blocks far below, sending up plumes of white water that the wind caught and snatched away before they had a chance to fall.

Bronwyn landed on the boardwalk and ran, ducking low to dodge the wind. Ash reached the bottom rung and followed after her. He had to reach the shack. He needed to check his plan with Mason, but time was against him.

As soon as I know the idea's not completely crazy I'll—

Something heavy slammed into his back, knocking the breath from his lungs. He hit the boardwalk hard and rolled over.

Dain stood above him, and the sky overhead was fit for the end of the world.

'Where do you think you're going, *boy*?'

Ash twisted his head, searching for Bronwyn, but she was already gone. The boardwalk was empty. He tried to shout but couldn't, and the small, choked sound that escaped his throat was quickly stolen by the wind. He turned back to Dain.

'You—' Ash croaked. He tried to get up but Dain pinned him beneath a boot.

'You know, I don't think there'd be too many questions asked if someone was to lose their footing on the boardwalk tonight.' Dain peered at the restless water below, black even in the brilliant flashes of light. 'No one would even hear the splash.'

Ash fought to wriggle free but Dain dug his heel into Ash's sternum.

'What have you got planned, boy? I heard you up there, hollering about bringing down the Wall. Tell me now and perhaps I can prevent the Warden from going too far.'

The breath caught in Ash's throat, and it had nothing to do with the pressure on his chest. The look on his face clearly delighted Dain, who began to smile.

'Don't looked so shocked, boy. Who better to keep the Warden informed than the man recruiting troublemakers for a rebellion?'

There was something about being called 'boy' that was like having a fistful of hair yanked repeatedly. All his life Ash had been a boy: a boy forced to fumble his way – fatherless – to manhood. It made Ash all the more determined to live, to outgrow his past. But he needed more time. He had to keep Dain talking.

'Why?' Ash said. 'Why wouldn't you want to escape the Wall?'

'And go back to the old life? Living hand to mouth? Scavenging?' Dain shook his head. 'No.'

'How is this life any better?'

Dain's smile widened. His black beard twitched in the wind, and the knucklebone buttons of his tunic gleamed with each pulse of lightning.

'You don't seem to understand,' he said. 'The Warden and I have an agreement, and when he hears about the plot I've foiled tonight, it won't be long till I'm carrying one of those fancy swords myself.'

The thought made Ash's stomach turn. He glanced along the boardwalk, hoping that someone might emerge from one of the shacks, but the storm kept everyone huddled inside.

'Do you really think you can trust a man like the Warden?' Ash said.

Dain's smile faded, and his stare turned cold and stony. 'He's always been a man of his word.'

There was something in Dain's expression, or his choice of words, or the deliberate way in which he spoke them, that made Ash very afraid. He remembered Robin insisting that Quinn hadn't been on watch the night Last Village was raided – even though Dain had claimed the opposite – and he realised just how depraved the man above him truly was. It was like finding himself on the edge of a deep well that seemed to go down for ever.

'You were the one on watch, weren't you? You let them into the village.' Ash was seized by a sudden rage, and he fought to get up. Dain increased the pressure on his chest. 'Why? How could you?'

Dain shrugged. 'You get to hear things, out on watch. You meet people from outside the village. People who have more to offer than a witch in a hilltop house.'

The wind dropped momentarily, and in the stillness Ash became certain that it was Dain who had killed Helena. This time, Ash fought so hard that he very nearly got free.

'That's enough!' Dain said, increasing the pressure on Ash's chest until he lay still.

'You're right. That is enough.'

Ash looked to the side and saw Mason standing several yards away with Bronwyn at his side.

'Let him go,' Bronwyn said.

Dain shook his head. 'Can't do that, I'm afraid. The Warden will be wanting a word with this one.'

Mason took a step forward, but Dain reached down and hauled Ash to his feet in one swift movement. Ash fought to find his footing, but it was all he could do to keep his toes on the edge of the board. His body was out over the water. Dain held him there, with Ash's tunic clutched in two powerful fists. Instinct forced Ash to cling to his captor.

'Take another step and this one goes the same way as his precious priestess.'

Mason stopped.

Dain's eyes gleamed with cruel mirth as they met Ash's. 'Tell me what you've got planned!'

'Don't tell him!' Bronwyn said.

Ash held Dain's gaze. Then he looked up at the sky. Dark clouds boiled over the top of the Wall. Time was running out.

'Okay,' he said. 'I will. But before I tell you, I want to know whether you betrayed my father. Did you know those men who took him? Was it you who made sure he was on watch the night they came to the village?'

Dain's smile widened. 'You're a lot like him, you know? Your father had a habit of asking troublesome questions.' He raised his chin and looked down at Ash with imperious eyes. 'It made the rumours of his desertion that much easier to believe.' He tightened his grip on Ash's shirt. 'Now, tell me what you're planning. It's not like you've got a choice.'

Ash glanced at Bronwyn and Mason, so close and yet powerless to help. High above, a bolt of lightning struck the cage in a spray of sparks, illuminating every crease and pore and bristle of Dain's smirking face.

Ash made up his mind.

'You're right,' he said. 'I don't have a choice.'

He threw his weight backwards. The sudden shift took Dain by surprise: he was slow to release his grip. By the time he realised he should let go it was already too late.

Another flash of lightning showed them at the point of no return. Mason and Bronwyn lunged forwards. But when the next pulse of light came, less than a second later, the space before them was empty.

Only the image of the falling figures remained, seared on their retinas, branded on to their brains.

21

The darkness was absolute, and so was Ash's disorientation. He needed to reach the surface but there was no way of knowing which way was up and which way was down: it could have been an inch above his head or ten yards below his feet. If he kicked out, as his legs longed to do, he might send himself further into the depths. Or he might collide with the Wall. The thought of something as monstrous as the Wall being concealed underwater made him wonder what else might be lurking in the gloom.

He cast about, his eyes and lungs stinging, searching for any indication of the surface. A flash of lightning lit the sky, and the black water turned blue-green. A solitary bubble passed before Ash's face, travelling upwards, and beyond that, close enough to send a shiver of terror through his body, was the Wall. Darkness swallowed him once more but he kicked out, following the bubble's path.

He broke the surface moments later. The gasp of air burned his lungs. He reached out a hand to stop himself from being swept into the Wall. The lapping waves were white-tipped and boisterous, each one determined to dash him against the stone blocks. He pushed off, kicking hard against the driving waves until he was safely away from the Wall.

Dain suddenly emerged beside him in an eruption of water, blind and panicky. His arms wheeled around in wild circles. He coughed.

'Save me!' he shouted. 'Four Fathers, save me!' He slipped beneath the waves. Popped up again. Spluttered. 'Save me!'

He sank once more. Ash watched the surface, treading water. He felt something brush against his ankle – groping fingers that sent a chill from his heels to the nape of his neck – then nothing.

He swam, fearful that those cold hands would grab him and pull him under. Even when enough time – more than enough time – had passed, he kicked with the horror of the unknown beneath and behind and ahead of him. The Wall was a constant, unnerving presence beside him, like the flank of an immense monster. His woollen clothes grew heavy. His arms began to tire. The gruelling day of labour and the constant jostling of rowdy waves began to take their toll. His gasping mouth filled with water. He choked and spluttered and slipped beneath the surface. He kicked, came up again, caught half a breath, and struggled on.

Finally, his right hand dragged through something soft that crammed in under his nails. He reached out with his left hand and felt stones, tangled grass, mud. He gave a final kick and felt his chest brush against earth. He had reached the eastern bank. He wound a clutch of flailing grass around his hand and held himself out of the water, panting. He did not look at the bank, not yet. It was steep: that was all he knew. The climb would be hard, and he needed a few moments to steel himself. He looked back and saw the Wall stretching away into darkness.

He breathed deeply. He could hear nothing but the wild wind and distant thunder and the chuckle of waves as they slopped against the bank. He pulled himself up out of the water. He crawled at first, the wind pummelling him and trying to rip the clothes from his back, but then he rose to his feet and staggered up the slope. He braced himself against the elements as best he could, but the wind knocked him to his knees again and again. He checked the sky; he had to move quickly if his plan were to have any chance of succeeding. He kept going.

By the time he reached the crest of the hill and finally looked back he was shaky and breathless. He was exhausted, but the sight of the water far below made him euphoric. He was off the Wall. He had escaped – just as his father had.

But there was still work to do.

The wind was even more fitful and contrary in this high, exposed place. He looked about at the scattering of round boulders and tried to forget the betrayal he had experienced here. He hurried over to the low cave, half expecting to find Samuel cowering inside, but it was empty.

Almost empty.

He ducked under the entrance and made his way to the back. It was too dark to see clearly, and so he fumbled along the fissures in the stone until his fingers touched something smooth and yielding: a satchel. It was empty. He reached out again and found the waterskin. He removed the stopper and drank the musty, leathery mouthful it contained. He cast it aside. His eyes began to adjust to the gloom, and finally he saw it: a pale brick, partly concealed beneath a grubby woollen blanket. He lifted it and carefully placed it in the empty satchel, looping the strap over his chest. A flash of lightning lit up the cave, and Ash saw the iron poles they had found in the mines and used as weapons and walking staffs. He snatched one up.

He turned, and was just about to head back into the maelstrom when something caught his eye. It was Kelly's club: the one he had found in Last Village. He wondered why Samuel hadn't taken it, as he had taken all the food. Perhaps weapons made his show of innocence harder to believe. He picked it up and tucked it into his belt.

Ash stood in the mouth of the cave and looked out at the writhing sky. Thunderclouds prowled above the reservoir, moving north in a restless mass of energy. He hefted the iron pole in his hand, like a hunter judging a throw. Then he stepped out and turned north, setting off along the spine of the ridge at a run.

He no longer felt the exhaustion in his limbs, did not feel the weight of the things he carried. Every step he took was one further from the Wall and closer to his goal. The Wall already felt imaginary: a dream place that one can recall but never return to. But he knew it was real – the callouses on his palms and the sinewy flesh of his arms were proof of it – and he knew he would have to go back.

He strode on, steering a course along the ridge. To be free, in a high place, running the gauntlet of the elements, was exhilarating. He thought, perhaps, that this might be how it felt to be a bat or a bird, or whatever that swooping, wheeling slice of night had been during the downpour. On and on he ran, through that narrow corridor between earth and sky, never looking back, never looking down.

Ash fixed his eyes on the northern edge of the lake: a thin crest of white marked the place where the dark water met the darker shore. The ridge began to curve around, and as it did so he caught a glimpse of the distant Kingdom, somehow still aglow with golden light.

He ran harder, only stopping when the Wall was a pale mark to the south. The vast lake lay in between: water that should have been flowing freely, winding its way between mountains and along valleys, until it eventually trickled into a pool at the foot of a small village he had once called home. It had not been a place of comfort or kindness, but it had been his home nonetheless. The place where his mother and father had lived, the place he had been born, the place that had made him the person he was now.

It should have been his home still.

And it will be my home again.

He made his way down from the rocky ridge, towards the lake. He did not want to go too far: he needed to be as high up as possible. He felt the ground with his hands, looking for the place where the rocks became earth. When he had found the spot he set the satchel down and began to dig, lifting the iron pole in both hands and bringing it down repeatedly, until the ground between his feet was broken and churned. He dropped to his knees and scooped out great clumps of cool earth with his hands. Overhead, the storm rumbled and fizzed and cracked and boomed, moving closer all the time.

When Ash finally had a hole that looked deep enough, he reached into the satchel and removed the pale, dense brick. He turned it over in his hands, then set it down in the bottom of the pit. Then he grasped the iron pole and gently worked the tapered end into the compacted powder. When it was embedded, he kicked dirt back into the hole and tamped it down with his feet. He took a quick step backwards, glad that the task was complete, and waited. The pole remained standing.

Then he clambered up, towards the ridge, and ran as fast he could.

Towards the Wall.

The wind intensified: it jostled and pummelled and yanked and shoved. It came at Ash from all angles, launching him forwards, pushing him sideways, driving him back. But Ash kept going. All his life he had been forced to struggle, to resist hands bent on dragging him to the ground. But now it wasn't only his survival that he fought for: it was everyone's. Everyone who had been taken to the Wall and everyone who ever would be. And he was determined not to fail them.

He reached the cave and began his descent towards the Wall, just as he had all those weeks ago, escorted by the Warden and his guards. He took the slope at a run, knowing how little time he might have to reach the bell. He did not stop to check whether any of the guards sheltering in the gatehouse were on watch; instead, he flew past its glowing windows, on to the Wall, and fought to keep his balance as the wind made a final attempt to knock him down.

Dark, churning clouds filled the sky in every direction, and the thunder was loud enough to make Ash's insides tremble. Little pulses of lightning danced through the clouds, bathing the Wall in intermittent, ghostly light.

Ash ran the last few steps to the bell and seized the

rope in his hand. He stood, panting, watching the northern shore of the lake through flailing strands of hair – waiting for the perfect moment.

'Come on,' he muttered to himself, hoping that it would work. Hoping that Bronwyn had managed to alert everyone. 'Come on.'

'I hope you're not praying to your gods.'

Ash spun around. The Warden stood in the centre of the Wall, a dark cloak billowing fitfully about him. He inhabited the violence like a conjuror, as though it was his creation, as though it would cease with a word or a gesture. A flash of lightning revealed him more fully, hatless and sinister and smirking, before the gloom shrouded him once more.

'Because they aren't listening. They don't even exist. All that exists – for you – is the Wall.'

Ash clung to the rope. He glanced over his shoulder, but only for a moment: he couldn't trust the Warden any longer than that.

'You're perilously close to the edge, Ash. Why don't you come here? Come here and I'll tell you things about your father – things you never got to know.'

Ash clamped his teeth together and braced himself against the storm. He knew the Warden was goading him, trying to lure him away from the bell, even if he didn't yet know why he clung to it. And he was very close to succeeding.

'Last chance,' the Warden said. He made it sound like a reasonable request. But then he drew his sword. He held it by his side, the point angled to the ground.

Ash glanced over his shoulder once more. Was the thunder receding? Were the lightning strikes growing less frequent?

He became convinced that his plan was going to fail. As he turned back to face the Warden, Ash caught sight of the cage and knew what awaited him.

He let go of the rope, defeated. The next gust nearly knocked him down. He staggered, determined to stay strong as his father would have done.

'Over there,' the Warden said, pointing to the opposite side of the Wall with the tip of his sword.

Ash obeyed, and as he did so the Warden moved to stand between him and the bell.

'Turn around,' the Warden said.

Ash frowned. The Warden took a step closer and raised the sword so that it pointed at Ash's chest.

Ash turned around to face the emptiness. He saw the dark shape of the Pikes, their ragged peaks lost within the thunderclouds. The empty space in between yawned like an open grave.

'Do you remember what I said the day you were brought here, Ash? About those who attempt to leave the Wall?'

Ash did remember and he realised, with a feeling too crushing to be described as relief, that he was not destined for the cage. Instead, he was about to be shown the fastest route off the Wall.

He nodded; he doubted whether his voice would carry with his back turned and his heart in his throat and the wind thrashing about.

'Well,' the Warden said. 'What are you waiting for? Are you going to make me push you?'

Ash closed his eyes and felt the wind against his eyelids. He took a deep breath. And then the wind dropped to nothing. The hairs on his arms stood up as a fizzing, tingling energy filled the air. He remembered how the pressure had dropped that last night with Helena, looking over the valley from the back door of the House on the Hill – the night before everything changed. He remembered the violence that followed.

He opened his eyes. He could feel the blade at his back. It wasn't close enough to touch him, but he could *sense* it.

He turned to face the Warden. The tip of the sword hovered inches away from Ash's heart.

'On my way here, I met someone who told me something I didn't know about myself. Something you're about to find out.'

The Warden raised a mocking eyebrow. 'And what would that be?'

Ash could almost hear the air crackling around him. Goosebumps travelled along his spine and across his scalp. When he answered, he spoke to the sky.

'That I was forged in fire.'

The thunder rose to new levels of raucousness. The clouds flashed white in a dozen places. And then a blistering arc of lightning splintered across the sky, white-hot and supercharged. It spread over the lake and plummeted towards the northern bank.

A piercing point of light lit up the landscape.

And then the explosives detonated with a muffled boom. The ground swelled and collapsed as though a buried giant were drawing breath. Another pulse of lightning illuminated a broad shower of debris.

And then the ground began to slip.

The entire northern bank came free and rushed towards the edge of the lake: a churning landslide of earth and rocks and boulders. It hit the water in a dark froth of foam, sending an enormous swell out into the lake. As it spread it began to rise, as though displaced by the back of some huge, cruising beast as it neared the surface.

And it was headed for the Wall.

'What have you done?' the Warden shouted. He had spun around at the sound of the explosion, and as he turned back Ash ducked behind him and ran to the bell. He grabbed the rope and rang it with all his might. Half a dozen clamorous peals filled the air before an arm clamped around his throat and dragged him backwards. He could see the approaching surge of water, building with every second that passed. He thought of what would happen if it struck the Wall while the shacks were occupied, and shivered.

What if they couldn't hear the bell over the storm? What if they didn't believe Bronwyn? What if there's not enough time to get everyone to safety?

But then heads began to appear over the edge of the Wall, and soon dozens of people were clambering over the top. The Warden edged backwards, pulling Ash with him, until his heels were at the very edge. He lifted his free hand to the side and placed the blade of the sword against Ash's throat. The sight stopped the evacuees in their tracks.

'Go!' Ash shouted. 'Run!'

He could see they didn't want to leave him, but one look at the coming tsunami left them with no choice. They fled.

Half a dozen guards had emerged from the gatehouse, swords drawn, but as soon as they saw the approaching wall of water they, too, turned and ran.

'Cowards!' the Warden shouted, tightening his grip on Ash's neck.

Mason appeared on the Wall, his fists clenched, and advanced on the Warden.

'One more step and I'll end him,' the Warden snarled.

Ash hissed as the sword nicked his skin and drew blood. Mason hesitated. Bronwyn appeared on the Wall and ran to his side.

'Let him go!'

The Warden laughed; his breath was hot in Ash's ear.

'The Wall is going to collapse!' Bronwyn said.

'You are wrong,' the Warden said. 'The Wall is strong: it will not fail.'

'You'll both be killed!' Mason shouted. 'Don't be a fool!'

The Warden shook his head. 'Only one of us is going to die today, and it will not be me.'

'Go!' Ash shouted. The bulge of water drew nearer, rising all the time. 'Help the others and go!'

Bronwyn looked at the Warden, her jaw set, eyes sharp. 'You are a mad dog. You don't know when to let go of the thing between your teeth.'

She looked at Ash, her eyes ablaze and full of unspoken meaning, before turning to help the last few people off the ladders. Then she cast a final look back at Ash and set off with Mason for the eastern bank.

Ash coughed and tried to swallow but the Warden's arm was clamped tight enough to choke him. It pressed against a lump that had not been there a few months earlier and Ash realised, with a stab of regret, that he was on the cusp of manhood but would go no further: if his plan worked, he would die; if his plan failed, he would die.

The thought filled him with a strange sense of calm. He watched the mighty surge of water as though it had already annihilated him. He released his grip on the Warden's chokehold and allowed his hands to fall to his sides.

His fingertips brushed against something smooth –

something that did not belong to him. Something that had, in its lifetime, been used to stun a hundred sheep.

And one mad dog.

Bronwyn's parting words suddenly made sense. Ash tiptoed his fingers along the shaft of Kelly's club and grasped the handle.

The wave rushed towards the Wall, silent and swift and colossal. Ash felt the Warden tense. He held his breath.

Ash waited until the moment of impact before swinging the club upwards in a short, vicious arc. The Warden's nose crumpled in an eruption of hot blood. He screamed in pain. Ash wriggled away from his loosened grip but was immediately knocked to his knees. The Wall shook beneath him as the tide of water smashed against it, spurting upwards in a veil of white foam.

For a moment, the Wall was a solid, immovable thing. But then the vast blocks turned weightless, began to shift and pivot like driftwood caught on a current, and the world began to tilt – to fall. A gap appeared between Ash's block and the one beside it. He scrambled forwards, fighting to find his balance as more and more stones began to move.

Ash leapt up on to the next block but, as he did so, a

hand grabbed the back of his tunic and brought him down. He turned over. The Warden lay behind him, his face a mess of blood and malice. With one hand he clutched Ash's tunic; with the other, he raised his sword.

'You!' he said.

He brought the sword down. Ash raised his club and deflected the blade. It fell from the Warden's hand and slid along the block, dropping into a gap between the stones. Great jets began to erupt on the southern side of the Wall as the water found chinks and turned them into chasms.

'Let go!' Ash shouted. He could feel himself beginning to slide on the tilted block, towards nothingness. 'Let me go!'

He lashed out with the club, bringing it down on the Warden's wrist. Ash heard the crack above the roar and crunch of crumbling stone. The Warden yelped, clutching his floppy hand to his chest. Ash scrambled away, upwards, and leapt for the edge of the next block. He caught it with his fingertips, but already he could feel it listing towards the valley floor far below.

'Here!'

Ash looked up; Bronwyn stood above him. Ash reached out, and no sooner had his hand found hers than she began to pull him up. As he rose above the lip of the next block he saw that Mason held her other hand, and beyond him was Jane, and beyond her was Quinn, and then Robin, and then countless others, in a human chain that stretched towards the eastern end of the Wall.

Ash glanced back, just in time to see the Warden claw at a block with his useless hand. With a scream, he dropped into the chaos of water and stone below and was gone.

'Come on!' Bronwyn shouted.

They ran, jumping from stone to stone as they shifted and slipped and fell away. Above the pounding in his ears, Ash heard the furious, awesome sound of escaping water. It was the noise that scared him most, the thing that seemed impossible to escape, the thing that threatened to swallow him whole. He had never suspected that water could be so loud. He leapt from one block to the next, staggering and stumbling.

The water was going to claim him.

The water was going to seize him and carry him and dash him against the ground far below.

The water was going to succeed where everyone and everything up till now had failed.

It was incensed – enraged – and it would not be denied.

But then the stones beneath his feet grew more stable. He found his balance, and with it came a new hope of life, a fresh spurt of speed. Moments later, he was running towards the deserted gatehouse at full pelt, matching Bronwyn stride for stride. He didn't stop until he had reached the hillside beyond, where he collapsed next to the others and turned to see the destruction he had caused.

The huge stone blocks that had taken so long to quarry and move and lift and stack tumbled into the valley below. Water poured through the vast gap they had left in a mighty cascade, filling the air with a dense, drenching mist.

And that sound. That sound was like a roar of defiance.

22

The storm passed soon after. The people slept on the hilltop, out in the open. Too exhausted to climb, Ash was carried up by Mason and set down on a fleece blanket in the cave. They set sentries, fearful of the escaped guards, but those men had fled and would not come back. The night was still and warm and calm.

They woke to a spectacular sunrise: golden light that revealed the extent of the wreckage. A staircase of blocks remained on either side of the valley, but the centre of the Wall had been completely demolished. There were no shacks, no ladders, and no cage. The torrent of water had slowed; soon it would return to its natural flow. Huge blocks lay where the overseers' settlement had once stood: what remained of the buildings could have been carried by hand. The rest had been washed away.

Ash rose and emerged from the cave. He moved amongst the others as if in a dream. They let him pass.

Nobody spoke. He stopped at the edge of the summit, high above the ruins, and looked out over the landscape.

The sun rose higher. Golden light flooded the world, and the world, it seemed, was a flood of golden light. The burst dam had spread its waters over the plain below, and the surface shone like a sheet of glass. Out in the distance, a blazing thread wound its way between the mountains. The sight took Ash's breath away. He knew that far to the south, hours or days from now, a small pool in a village at the end of the world would begin to refill. The water was finding its way home, and Ash longed to do the same.

The sight before him, and the image in his mind, kept him from noticing the people who had come to stand beside him: one tall and hulking, the other small and slight.

'What do we do now?' Bronwyn asked.

Ash was still looking at the gilded landscape. He glanced at Mason, waiting for his reply, and was surprised to find Mason watching him. He turned to Bronwyn.

'You're asking me?' he said.

She grinned. 'Who else?'

Ash turned, and found that the people gathered behind him were all patiently awaiting his answer.

He swallowed. His eye caught the mess of broken stone in the valley below, then drifted to the flooded plain, the broken forest, the dark shape of the Pikes beyond.

'The Kings will come for us,' Mason said.

Ash nodded. The Kingdom's miraculous supply of water would be about to run dry, and he knew that they would come looking for whoever was responsible: he was sure of it because that is what he himself had done, all those months ago.

Ash looked at the bedraggled survivors behind him. And then he looked at the landscape once more. He thought of the others, out there. Not just the people he had met: the unknown others. Because there *would* be others, he was sure of it. Some would mean well, and some would mean harm, but they would all be frightened and alone and desperate for something better. For somewhere else to go. Just as the people behind him were.

Ash swallowed the lump in his throat.

'We need to find somewhere to regroup,' he said. 'Regroup and rebuild.'

'And the Kingdom?' Bronwyn asked.

Ash took a deep breath and set his jaw.

'Let the Kingdom come.'

Afterword

A few years ago, I began to ask myself some questions about the future of this planet, a future that may well be defined by climate collapse:

What would it be like to live in a world without seasons — a sweltering, suffocating world where only the hardiest species survive: rats and sheep and humans?

What if the future is not a high-tech utopia as we often like to imagine, but medieval and meagre and monstrous?

What stories would the survivors of this future tell about their ancestors — us — and the world we bequeathed to them?

This last question is the one that haunted me most. I suspected that the truth — that we simply cared more about ourselves than our children — would not make sense to them. It goes against nature, which is why we are beginning to experience a world of unnatural disasters. And so I began to write *Spark*, creating a world that our actions (and inaction) could feasibly lead towards. I devised a primitive belief system for the people of Last Village, wherein our mindless destruction of the planet is mistaken for an arbitrary, godlike power, and the villagers are left seeking forgiveness for what are in fact their ancestors' crimes. Through their ignorance and denial and fear we, the villains, are redrawn as heroes.

The perspective that these questions create – that of looking back at ourselves from an imagined future – is an extremely powerful one. It reminds us that there will probably be people who witness the exhaustion of resources long thought to be infinite, and the loss of species presumed to be too numerous to exterminate. There will be people. Remember that. There will be people, and we are in the process of deciding what kind of lives they will live.

I wrote much of *Spark* during the Covid-19 pandemic. It was a miserable time by most reckonings but the lockdowns in the UK – especially the first one in the spring of 2020 – gave us a glimpse of the drastic changes we need to make to avoid the bleak climate scenarios that are being forecast: planes grounded, roads deserted, a new appreciation of the natural world. Encouragingly, it did not take long for wildlife to creep back on to the stage in a silent encore. But we must give nature that chance. We must make space for the rest of life. There will be no sense of victory in being the last animals left alive on planet Earth. And that is why we must change before the climate does. We still have that power: *you* still have that power.

You have power as long as you are alive, which means that you – as a young person – have more power than most.

So use it. Use it now. Use it for good, or lose it for good.

Mitch Johnson, 2021

Acknowledgements

I originally intended to set *Spark* in the Lake District, and although the specifics have been lost the book retains many features and echoes of that landscape. I would not have been able to conduct my research trip to Cumbria without the generosity and hospitality of Nick and Sophie Anderson and their family – thank you for giving me a place to stay. The sequence set in the mines was inspired by a visit to Honister Slate Mine and I would wholeheartedly recommend a tour to anyone lucky enough to be in the area. (You won't need to arm yourself, but a coat might be a good idea.) Many thanks to Tori for showing me around and answering all my questions. The House on the Hill is loosely based on Beatrix Potter's house; thanks to the guides at Hill Top for your expertise and allowing me to photograph pretty much everything.

Thanks to the scientists, activists, artists and authors

who are working tirelessly to turn the tide before it engulfs us. I read many books whilst researching *Spark* but the depictions of climate disaster in Mark Lynas's *Six Degrees* and David Wallace-Wells's *The Uninhabitable Earth* were especially useful/terrifying.

Thanks to everyone at Hachette Children's Group who helped to bring this book into the world. Special thanks to my editor, Tig Wallace, for trusting me to rewrite half the book (twice) and for making so many wise suggestions along the way. You would be an Elder of Last Village for sure. Thanks to Ruth Girmatsion and Helen Hughes for getting *Spark* over the finish line, and to Flic Highet and Lucy Clayton for shouting from the hilltops about it. Thanks to Lynne Manning for creating another electrifying cover, and to Matt Schu for the artistic wizardry. Thanks also to Belinda Jones for spotting so many errors and wringing every last drop of tension from the manuscript.

Thanks to Caz for keeping me company in what would otherwise have been a terribly dreary workspace: our book chats were a happy distraction from the mountain of words that lay before me.

Thanks to my agent, Felicity Trew, for all your help in navigating these strange times and for always knowing what to do for the best. I'm pretty sure there's a village somewhere missing its High Priestess . . .

Finally, thanks to Harrie, Evie and Olive for getting me through the lockdowns and low points. You make me laugh and smile and remind me that there are more important things in the world than work. Thank you for being beacons of light whenever I lose my spark.

ALSO BY MITCH JOHNSON

An outrageous theft. A huge reward. Two friends on the run. An uproariously funny, action-packed adventure about the power of courage, standing up for what's right, and fizzy drinks.

Queenie stares out at the ocean and dreams of a world beyond her small town. She's about to get her wish . . . When the priceless recipe to the world's most popular drink – thought to be lost forever – washes up at her feet, Queenie's life instantly changes. Everyone wants it, and with a $10 million bounty on her head, Queenie's soon on the run.

Pursued by bounty hunters, black-ops helicopters and angry mobs, Queenie's journey involves a trip to Area 51, a man-eating alligator and an unlikely new friend. But being on the run also makes Queenie see the world around her more clearly – a world in which a big corporation's excess has left the planet covered in plastic bottles and waste. Suddenly, the home she always dreamed of escaping, and the ocean she grew up with and took for granted, don't seem so bad.

If Queenie and Todd can bring down the bad guys, maybe she can go back home and make a difference . . .

'FIZZES WITH ADVENTURE AND GREAT CHARACTERS WHO POP FROM THE PAGE'
- PETER BUNZL, BESTSELLING AUTHOR OF COGHEART

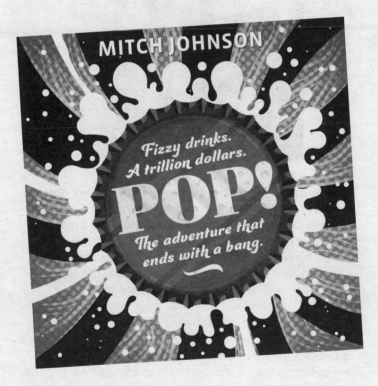

After graduating from the University of East Anglia with an award-winning degree in English Literature with Creative Writing, Mitch completed *Kick*, his debut novel for middle-grade readers. Endorsed by Amnesty International UK for its portrayal of children's rights, *Kick* also received the 2018 Branford Boase Award.

For Mitch, books are a means of activism as well as entertainment, which is why he tends to write stories of social injustice infused with warmth and humour. He believes books should not just create new worlds, but help us to dream up new ways of looking at the one in which we live.

Mitch now works as a Waterstones bookseller in Norwich where he lives with his wife and daughters.